This is the worst idea ever, a voice in the back of her head whispered.

She ignored the voice. There was no time for second-guessing or doubt or making another choice. There was only trust that Angel would get her out of this mess with her skin intact.

He'd done it so far.

He gunned the bike, and she clutched at him as they roared through the open doorway. Behind them, men yelled and gunfire sounded over their shouts. Fiona flinched, expecting to feel a bullet in the back with each passing heartbeat. She glued herself to Angel until there wasn't even air between them and prayed their luck would last.

"Hang on!" he shouted.

As if she needed to be told.

Dear Reader,

I am a bit of a traveler. In fact, I have a hard time staying put in one geographical region for more than a year at a time. For me, travel is a way to learn about other cultures, ideas, world events and more. It also influences me as a writer. Archaeological sites, places, people and even tension in the air are fodder for my imagination.

The seed for *Mercenary's Honor* came from my time in Oaxaca, Mexico. In 2006, I wanted to get away. I picked Mexico because my Uncle Jim lives there, and I thought it would be nice to have someone close on foreign soil. So off I went. Just in time for the riots.

Yes—riots.

I touched down just as teachers marched on the city (it's how they get their raise each year), and then the Mexican presidential election began. I saw burning buses, got caught up in a peaceful demonstration—and managed to cross a metal barrier just before a non-peaceful demonstration broke out.

A few months into this chaos, a reporter was killed. A stray bullet, I believe. I began to think about reporters who typically go into areas in conflict. How do they do it? What if they see something they shouldn't—what would they do?

Thus, *Mercenary's Honor* was born. I hope you enjoy the book, and if you look, I think you'll see a little bit of my adventures in the pages.

—Sharron

Mercenary's HONOR
Sharron McClellan

Silhouette®
Romantic
SUSPENSE

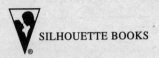

SILHOUETTE BOOKS

ISBN-13: 978-0-373-27600-4
ISBN-10:   0-373-27600-1

MERCENARY'S HONOR

Visit Silhouette Books at www.eHarlequin.com

Printed in U.S.A.

Books by Sharron McClellan

Silhouette Romantic Suspense

Mercenary's Honor #1530

Silhouette Bombshell

The Midas Trap #29
Hidden Sanctuary #114

SHARRON McCLELLAN

began writing short stories in high school but became sidetracked from her calling when she moved to Alaska to study archaeology. For years, she traveled across the United States as a field archaeologist specializing in burials and human physiology. Between archaeological contracts, she decided to take up the pen again. She completed her first manuscript two years later, and it was, she says, "A disaster. I knew as much about the craft of writing as Indiana Jones would know about applying makeup." It was then that she discovered Romance Writers of America and began serious study of her trade. Three years later in 2002, she sold her first novel, a fantasy romance. Sharron now blends her archaeological experience with her love of fiction as a writer for the Silhouette Romantic Suspense line. To learn more, visit her at www.sharronmcclellan.com. She loves to hear from her readers.

To my mom and dad. For instilling a love of reading
in me and encouraging my writing. I appreciate
the time, the help, but mostly, I appreciate your belief
that I would be a success.

ACKNOWLEDGMENTS

Many thanks to James McClellan (Uncle Jim!) and
Antonio Reyes of Casa Adobe B&B (Oaxaca, Mexico)
for the Spanish translations.

Chapter 1

"He won't kill her," Fiona whispered, adjusting the dark scarf that covered her bright blond hair. "He can't."

It was early morning with the sun barely over the horizon. She and her cameraman, Anthony Torres, lay flat on a fourth-floor balcony with only blooming bougainvillea and an ancient black wrought-iron railing for cover.

Peeking through the cover of leaves, thorns and purple blossoms, they watched the courtyard below where Ramon Montoya, head of Colombian National Security, was interrogating Maria Salvador. According to rumor, she was one of the leaders of *Revolucionarios Armados de Colombia*—RADEC—a rebel group dedicated to freeing Colombia from the iron grip of the current regime—of which Montoya was the worst.

"It's not like it would be his first execution." Tony kept the small camera focused on the scene.

"Really?"

"Yeah, really," Tony said, not taking his eyes off the scene below. "But he usually doesn't kill women. Not often."

Small comfort, Fiona thought, stifling a yawn.

"Do not tell me you're bored," Tony said.

"Not a chance," Fiona whispered. "But I could use a cup of espresso." They'd been hitting the sketchier bars for the past few nights searching for *the* story, the one that would make them both famous. Then, last evening, their diligence plus a fistful of American dollars had brought them here.

Fiona was thrilled to have the chance to report something worthwhile, but she would have been more thrilled if she'd had a few hours of sleep.

Beneath them, Montoya backhanded Maria across the face, the sound echoing against the brick enclosure. Maria fell to the ground in a small heap, her long black hair spreading across the broken pavement.

A shot of adrenaline surged through Fiona, dissipating her need for rest. "We have to stop him," Fiona whispered even as the reporter in her told her to stay put. To watch with dispassion and do her job.

"With what? Harsh words?"

Fiona rolled her eyes. "How about calling for help?"

"Call who? The police?" Tony asked with a hint of sarcasm.

She frowned, since the men below them were in charge of the police. "Someone. Anyone," she said with a scowl.

"See if my cell works," Tony said, rolling to his side a few inches but never losing the shot. "Front right pocket."

Fiona dug into his jeans pocket and wrapped her fingers around the phone.

"Farther down," he whispered with a wicked grin. "And firmer."

"Pervert." She pulled the cell out and flipped it open. It blinked at her, showing no coverage. Sometimes, she hated Third World countries. Granted, they had all the best stories, but at times like this she missed the United States and the convenience of a cell tower on every corner.

She shoved the phone back into Tony's pocket. "No signal."

"Not a sur—"

Maria screamed, cutting off Anthony. Fiona froze. Squinting in the sunlight, she watched as Montoya pulled the woman to her feet by her hair.

Bastard.

"¿Dónde están, Maria?" Montoya screamed the question—*where are they*—loud enough that Fiona was sure the neighboring country heard his shout. Yet none of the curtains in the windows surrounding the courtyard so much as fluttered. People didn't want to get involved, and she couldn't blame them. When the men in charge were the bad guys, there was no one to turn to.

That was why she was here, she reminded herself. To uncover the truth and help make changes in a country run by a government that was as corrupt as the Mafia and twice as dangerous. If she won an Emmy, or perhaps a Pulitzer, that was icing on the cake and nothing more.

Or so she told herself, even as she envisioned herself giving an acceptance speech.

The air in the courtyard tightened, became electric with tension. Montoya's men straightened.

Something was about to happen, she realized. Fiona pushed thoughts of a Pulitzer to the back of her mind and strained to listen.

Maria said something, but her husky voice carried no farther than Montoya's ears. He drew closer. She spat on him. He wiped her spit off his cheek.

"Good for her," Fiona whispered, but she hoped that Maria's small act of defiance wouldn't cost her.

"I'm not so sure," Tony replied. He tweaked the directional microphone and adjusted his earpiece. It wasn't large, but Fiona knew it was the most powerful sound device on the market and it picked up sounds that she couldn't hear.

"What's he saying?" she asked.

"That if she tells him where the rebels are he will make sure they are imprisoned but not killed."

"She doesn't buy that, does she?"

Tony hesitated. "No. She's still denying any involvement."

"What do you think?" Fiona asked, wondering if the woman was as innocent as she claimed. Not that it mattered. No one should be subjected to such brutality by the hands of those who were sworn to protect the public. "Is she uninvolved?"

"No," Tony whispered. "According to my contacts, she's at the top of that particular food chain."

Fiona's blood chilled. If Tony was so certain, it was a sure bet that Montoya was, as well. "Damn it."

"Exactly, but as long as she doesn't confess to anything, I think she'll be fine," Tony said.

Montoya hit Maria again, the force of the blow making her take a step back.

Fiona winced, wishing she was as sure as her cameraman. "I hope you're right," she whispered. "Because in a few seconds, I am going to have to say or do something."

"Hold your horses, Don Quixote," Tony cautioned. "I think something's happening." He adjusted the camera and zoomed in on the scene.

Below them, Montoya pushed Maria away and pointed toward a door on the far side of the courtyard. "Is he letting her go?" Fiona's heart pounded with fear and anticipation.

"It looks that way," Tony said, but his tone suggested the same lack of sureness that pulsed through Fiona.

Maria adjusted her tiered skirt, dusted the leaves from her hair and headed for the doorway with her head held high. The men moved aside to let her pass.

Fiona's pounding heart slowed, and she breathed a sigh of relief, letting her head drop to her hands. "Thank God," she whispered. Maria was going to be all right. They had the story, and she'd be able to sleep at night.

A barrage of gunshots sounded from the courtyard below, and Fiona snapped to attention, swallowing her shout of horror.

Through the bougainvillea, she saw Maria on the pavement. Bullet holes riddled her lithe body. Blood spattered the pavement around her.

Even as Fiona gaped in horror, Tony jumped to his feet. "No!"

Below, Montoya whirled, and even at forty feet, Fiona saw his eyes widen in surprise at the cameraman's appearance. In less time than it took her to realize what was happening, Montoya raised his gun and fired. Tony fell backward, striking the wall behind them as blood bloomed on his chest. His camera clattered to the tiled floor, still filming.

For a heartbeat, Fiona stared at him, stunned. Not sure whether he was alive or dead and not sure what to do in either case.

"Fiona," Tony whispered, his voice thick with pain.

His voice brought her back to reality. "Oh, my God, we've got to get you out of here."

He coughed and blood stained his lips. "Not going anywhere." Tony grabbed for the camera, missing. "Run. Take the film to Angel."

"Angel?" Hands shaking, Fiona moved the camera aside to check the wound. The entrance wasn't bad, she realized, but blood poured from beneath him from an exit wound she suspected was monstrous.

Tony grabbed her wrist. "Get to Angel. Mercenary. Friend." He strained to talk, his words clipped and tight. "He can protect you. The film."

Film? Who cared? "Screw the film." Fiona shook her head. "What the hell were you thinking? I have to get you to a doctor."

Remaining low and out of sight, she pressed one hand to his chest and another against his back. The feel of his blood, warm and sticky on her palms, made her nauseous.

Tony's eyelids fluttered and a whimper escaped his lips. "Stop," he whispered through clenched teeth. "Please. Stop."

"Oh, God. Oh, God. Oh, God," Fiona muttered. They'd hopped across rooftops to get to the building. How was she going to get him out if he couldn't walk?

"Angel. Get to Angel," Tony insisted.

"No." She pressed harder, but the blood refused to stop.

"Leave me or die."

"Fine. I'll go," she agreed, even though she did not intend to leave him alone. "Stubborn, butt-headed drama queen."

Though he labored to breathe, Tony managed a weak smile. "Not me. You," he said, his voice faint.

With the back of her hand, Fiona wiped away tears she'd been unaware of until they'd blurred her vision. Maybe if she found this Angel person, she could convince him to help her with Tony. "Where do I find him?"

"Tierra Roja."

The bar on the zocalo? It wasn't a surprise. What better place to find a mercenary? "I'll hurry," she said.

"Good." Tony touched her hand, his grip weak. "This makes me miss dog shows."

She twined her fingers through his. When she'd met Tony a few months ago, she was covering a dog show in Los Angeles, and he was her new cameraman. They'd bonded over the fact that they both thought their talents were wasted. Then he'd suggested they come to Colombia, his country, and find a story, make things happen instead of playing the game.

Some story.

"Me, too," she replied. "Though I could live without the constant leg-humping."

Tony gave a feeble chuckle. "That was my favorite part."

Shouting in the courtyard caught her attention. "Be right back," Fiona said. Letting go of his hand, she crawled back to the edge of the balcony and peered over. Montoya was yelling. Pointing.

Seconds later, the sound of a door splintering made her tremble. Montoya's men were in the building. They'd be on her in a few minutes. She'd have to hide Tony until she could come back with help. She crawled back to him. "I'll be back soon," she promised. "With Angel. I'm going to get you out of here."

She froze.

Tony stared at the sky. His chest no longer rose and fell. She swallowed back a cry of despair. "Tony?"

Nothing. She touched him. "Anthony?" He was dead. For a moment, she stared at the corpse, oblivious to anything but his sightless eyes. Then shouts reached her ears.

Montoya's men.

Panic roared through her body. She clenched her hands into tight fists. Focus, she told herself. Focus, Fiona. Focus or die.

Taking a deep, controlled breath, she forced the rising panic to the back of her mind then exhaled. Her pulse slowed. She unclenched her fists.

Time to run.

Wiping the blood off her palms and onto her denim-covered thighs, she closed Tony's eyes with a shaky hand, popped the microtape out of the camera and stuck it in the front pocket of her jeans.

Retracing the route she and Tony had taken to break in to the ancient apartment complex, she hunched over to keep her profile low and hurried through the French doors and into the empty hotel room. The sound of feet echoed in the stairwell. The men were almost at her floor.

Although it was risky to enter the open hallway, Fiona hurried across the few feet of the narrow passage and into the opposite room, easing the door shut behind her.

Out in the hallway, the men reached the fourth-floor landing.

Fiona ran for the window and swung both feet over the ledge. Dropping to the roof a few feet below her, she landed on her toes for silence. Even though she stood outside and with the door closed, the soldier's speech carried through the thin walls. She froze, listening.

"Esta vacío," someone shouted.

It's empty. They'd found the camera and checked.

"Encuentre a su socio."

Find his partner. They knew about her. *They knew.* She put her hand over her mouth to keep from throwing up.

Angel Castillo stared at the shot of mescal in front of him, debating if it was too soon in the day to have a drink. Wasn't it Alan Jackson who sang that it was "five o'clock somewhere"?

He picked up the shot glass and turned it around, letting the sunlight filter through the pale yellow liquid.

"Isn't it a little early for that?" Juan asked as he wiped down the top of the bar.

"Then why did you serve me?"

"Because you tip well."

Angel shrugged. His mother had been a waitress, working at a diner, and the nights she came home with little more than a few crumpled bills outnumbered the nights she came home with bulging pockets.

He knew the food business was difficult. Even more so when it was in a crap-hole like Bogotá, Colombia.

He set the glass down, and Juan slid a cup of coffee in front of him. "Try this."

"I've tasted your coffee. It's more lethal than any bullet."

"Yeah?" Juan laughed. "At least you'll be awake to hear the shot."

Angel shrugged and took a sip. The brew was thick. Black. And possibly illegal in some countries. If not, it should be.

"Bad night?" Juan asked as he put away glasses from last night's patrons, a combination of locals and tourists that never failed to amuse.

Angel glanced at Juan over the rim of the mug. A few weeks ago, when he'd come in at two in the morning, bleary-eyed and almost incoherent from lack of sleep, he'd told the bartender about the nightmares.

Mostly, Angel didn't remember them. He wasn't sure if that made them better or worse. What he did remember were the emotions they heaped on him. Anger. Remorse. The sense of helplessness.

"The dreams?" Juan pressed.

Angel raised a brow. This was the last time he confided in a bartender.

Juan shrugged. "Hey, if you need to talk, let me know."

"You going to ask me about my feelings next?" Angel asked. The corners of his mouth turned up a notch to show there was jest beneath the words. "Should we bond? Perhaps do each other's makeup, eat ice cream, and watch a Hugh Grant movie?"

Juan chuckled. "Kind of girlie to ask you if you want to talk, huh?"

Angel held his index and thumb an inch apart. "A notch."

"Blame it on Maria," Juan said. "She says we all should be more attuned to those around us."

Angel chuckled and sipped the coffee. Juan was smitten with the freedom fighter. Hell, everyone was smitten with her, and it wasn't just her beauty. It was true that her long wavy hair, dusky skin, and green eyes captured the attention of men, but her passion held it. Passion for her people. For her country. For the truth.

Maria was a force of nature, and while her enthusiasm for the

RADEC cause wasn't something he shared, he admired her for it. She inspired not just him but thousands of people.

He pushed the shot of mescal away. "I don't think I'll need this today."

Fiona crouched in an alley, watching the doorway of Tierra Roja and surprised to see movement inside before noon. It was hard to believe anyone would drink at ten in the morning, but this was Colombia. Sometimes, the only way to get through the day was with the edges of life a little blurred.

She looked up and down the street. Cars. People. Men with large guns. It was a day like any other in Bogotá.

Running her hands over her bloodstained jeans, she wished she could change clothes, but she didn't dare go back to her hotel. Montoya might not know who Anthony was—or his partner— but he'd figure it out. With her luck, sooner rather than later.

She stood, knees shaking. "Come on, Fiona," she whispered to herself. "Just get across the street, and you'll be safe."

Trying to appear nonchalant, she waited until the road was clear of traffic and hurried across. Without breaking pace, she pushed her way into the bar then slammed the door behind her. Taking a deep breath, she leaned against the scarred wooden slab.

"Are you well, *señorita?*" the bartender asked.

She glanced around the room. Other than the bartender, there was one other patron. Dressed in jeans, a black T-shirt and black boots, he had a cup of coffee and a shot of something in front of him.

He sipped the coffee, not showing any awareness she'd entered.

Great, a drunk, she thought, heading toward the far end of the bar. However, as she drew closer, she scrutinized him with a reporter's observational skills and had to admit he looked good for a drunk. Big. Muscled and in shape. Black hair clipped neat and short, but not military tight. A professional of some sort.

Angel perhaps? But he could just as easily be one of

Montoya's men. She stopped short, then realized she'd have to take a chance either way. She continued across the floor and leaned against the bar a few feet away. Closer still, she noticed there were circles beneath the man's eyes, and he drank the coffee as if it were the one thing keeping him alive.

He had to be Angel. He looked like the kind of man who might kill—or protect—for cash.

She shifted toward him. "Excuse me?"

He didn't acknowledge her. "Excuse me?" she said again, raising her voice and taking another step in his direction. "Angel?" she whispered, taking the chance he was the mercenary.

He sipped his coffee, showing no sign of recognition of the name. The pit in her stomach deepened.

"We are not open yet, *señorita*," the bartender said as he continued to hand-wash the bar glasses.

"Oh." She turned away from the dark man. "I don't want a drink." She went to the bartender. They were supposed to know everything. "I need a man," she whispered

He grinned. "Who do you want?"

Judging by the goofy expression on his tanned face, he thought she meant sex. Now was not the time for jokes. A vision of Anthony flashed across her eyes.

For what seemed like the millionth time since she ran away, she pushed the bloody image out of her mind and blinked back tears. Later, when the film was safe, she'd mourn. "Not like that. I need a specific man. He's called Angel. I was told he came here. A lot."

"Angel? I don't know him." The bartender shook his head, and his eyes remained on her, not sliding toward the dark man. Not even for a second.

Fiona's heart dropped. "I was told he came here," she insisted. Almost as if she floated outside her body, she heard her voice grow higher, more frightened and shaky. She didn't care. "I was told."

"You were told wrong," the bartender said, disentangling her hands from his shirt. "Let me get you a cup of coffee."

She hadn't realized she'd grabbed him. Fiona stuffed her hands into her pockets. Her fingertips touched Tony's footage, and she yanked that hand back out.

Taking a deep breath, she sat on a barstool and let her head drop to the wooden bar. This was not going well. Not at all.

"Here, you need this more than me," a deep voice said.

She raised her head in time to see the dark man slide his shot glass toward her. She stopped it before it sailed over the end of the bar. "It's not even noon."

"Suit yourself." He went back to his coffee.

She eyed the liquid. Though it was pale yellow in color, it still looked like something someone had made in their bathtub. And she was not much of a drinker, in any case. Still, she picked it up.

Tony flashed through her thoughts. His quick wit. His laugh. His bloody death. "Screw it," she whispered. Tipping her head back, she downed the shot.

Mescal, she realized as it burned a path down her throat. She put her hand over her mouth, a coughing fit doubling her over.

"Drink this." The bartender's voice cut through the hacking sound of her cough. After she caught her breath, she noticed the cup of coffee, with milk and sugar on the side, on the bar in front of her.

"Thanks," she said, adding the milk.

He patted her hands. "I'll get you something to eat."

"I'm not hungry," she said, her voice strangled as she fought back tears.

His eyes widened. "I insist," he said, disappearing into a back room.

It was the tears, Fiona thought as the door swung shut. It didn't matter the nationality, men freaked when a woman cried.

Fiona took a deep breath, shut her eyes, and assessed the

situation. She was on the run. It was a matter of hours, at best, before Montoya figured out who she was. She needed Angel. If she couldn't find him, she'd have to make her own way out of the country. For now, she'd assume the worst.

That she was on her own.

Okay. What do you do? she asked herself.

First, a disguise, she decided. She needed to hide herself. She touched the scarf that covered her head and realized it had slipped. She tried to fix it, but her shaking hands refused to cooperate. Frustrated, she yanked it off, wishing her hair was anything but blond. Dye would help, but there was no way she could conceal her fair skin and blue eyes. Hell, her height alone, just shy of six feet, made her an object of curiosity amongst the people in South America.

"Why do you want Angel?" the dark man asked, interrupting her thoughts.

Startled, Fiona spilled her coffee. The hot liquid spread across the bar and dripped onto her lap, making her hiss in pain. Great. "I was told he could help me," she said as she grabbed a handful of cocktail napkins to clean the mess.

"Help with what?" He turned to face her.

The dark circles beneath his eyes drew her initial attention, and she wondered if he ever slept. Her eyes slipped upward, past the smudges to his clear hazel eyes. He held her gaze, then his attention slid down her body, taking in everything from her head to her feet, including her bloody jeans. She let the wad of napkins drop to her lap, but no amount of coverage could hide the dark stains that soaked her from thigh to knee. Touching her hair, she brought his attention back to her face and away from her clothes. "I'll only talk to him," she replied, her tone aloof. "So unless you can tell me where he is, I can't say a word."

The man shrugged. "I might know. He doesn't like to be

bothered. What happened? Domestic problem?" His eyes went to her jeans again.

Domestic problem? Fiona swallowed back a hysterical giggle. "An accident."

"That's a lot of blood for an accident," he said. Rising from the barstool, he walked toward her.

He was tall, just over six feet three inches, and broad. Like a linebacker.

And as intimidating as one of Montoya's enforcers.

"Are you okay?" he asked.

She nodded. "It's not mine."

"Don't cry," he said.

"I'm not," she said, then realized she was doing exactly that. Tears slid down her cheeks, dripping onto the napkins covering her lap. She wiped her face with the back of her hand. "I'm sorry, it's just—" She stopped herself. What was she going to say?

That she'd watched a man, a friend, die?

Her eyes felt hot. Itchy. She willed the dark man to stop staring at her.

But he refused to turn away. "Tell me why you want Angel, and I'll see if I can find him."

She pressed her hand against the dark man's chest to steady herself. His heart beat strong against her palm. Warm. Alive.

The burden, the pain, was too great to bear any longer. She had to trust someone. Just a little. "I can't tell you, but if you find Angel, tell him that Anthony Torres sent me."

"Tony?" Recognition flashed across his eyes.

"You know him?"

The man nodded. For the third time, his eyes slid to her clothes. "Is Tony okay?"

Fiona tried to answer, but all that came out was a stuttered gasp as she tried to breathe.

It seemed to be enough of an explanation for the stranger. His eyes darkened, and she prayed he didn't direct his anger in her direction. Because if he did, she was dead. "Juan," he barked, "bring me another shot."

"No," came the muffled answer from behind the door.

The dark man leaned over the bar and grabbed the bottle of mescal.

Fiona shook her head. "I have to stay sober. They're after me." She clamped her hand over her mouth at the slip.

"Who? The men who killed Tony?"

Her head jerked up, and fear roared through her. *He knew.* Had she misjudged the man? Was he one of *them?* One of Montoya's men? She pushed away from him and stumbled from the chair, backing up toward the front door. "What do you mean? Who are you?" Her back met the painted cinderblock wall.

The man came toward her. Dark. Menacing. She couldn't move, no matter how much adrenaline pulsed through her blood. He reached for her, and she shut her eyes.

He pressed something into her hand.

She opened her eyes. Another shot. It was half full this time.

"Drink it," he insisted, taking her elbow and leading her back to the bar. "Then tell me what happened."

She'd said too much already. Given away too much. "I can't. I have to talk to Angel."

"You are."

Her breath caught in her throat. This was Angel? "Why didn't you say something?"

He didn't shrug. Nod. Or offer an explanation. But his expression softened. Angel leaned closer, and she saw a glimmer of something in his eyes.

Compassion. And it made her want to cry all over again.

"Tell me who killed Tony," he said.

Fiona rolled the shot between her palms. "Who killed him?" Montoya had pulled the trigger. Fired the bullet.

But *she'd* put Tony in danger. Pushed him. Talked him into doing something stupid. She straightened her shoulders. "For all practical purposes, it might as well have been me."

Chapter 2

He didn't believe her dramatic claim for a moment but Angel recognized the emotion behind it—guilt.

"It wasn't you," he said, taking the shot from her hand. "I know what killers look like." She didn't have it in her. Not even an iota. "And you're not it."

"It might as well have been," she whispered, but even as she argued, fatigue replaced the panic in her blue eyes as the adrenaline wore off. She wavered on her feet. Angel dropped the half shot, not caring that mescal sprayed across his boots.

Her eyes rolled backward, and he caught her in his arms before she hit the ground, one arm under her knees and the other across her back. While she was Amazon tall, she was lighter than she appeared, and carrying her across the room and laying her on one of the long tables was akin to zero exertion.

Leaning over her, he wondered what had happened. Gently, his fingertips skimmed her forehead as he pushed her hair away from her face. She was beautiful, with that perfect skin usually reserved for china dolls and airbrushed cover models.

She also knew Tony, which made her important. What was she to him? Friend? Revolutionary? Killer? Co-worker? Lover?

The last thought made him frown.

"Is she okay?" Juan asked, coming out from the back room.

"She's fine," Angel said. But what about Tony? He touched her bloodstained jeans. Her panic and fright told him that she wasn't a professional soldier, so if it was Tony's blood on her clothes, she might be wrong in her assessment of the situation. Tony might be hurt and nothing more.

Still, it was a helluva lot of blood.

Her eyelids fluttered.

"Give her this." Juan pressed a cup into his hand.

"What's in it?"

"More coffee. Black."

"Thanks."

"There's breakfast on the bar." He gave the woman a deliberate once-over. "A little food would do her good."

Angel wasn't so sure. She was thin, but in an athletic way. Not an underfed, someone-please-give-her-a-sandwich kind of way.

Before he could respond, the woman's eyes opened, and she pushed her elbows under her, sitting up halfway. "What happened?"

"You fainted."

"I fainted?" Her brows pressed toward each other, creating a furrow between them. "I've never fainted in my life."

"Tough morning," Angel said.

She squeezed her eyes shut, and for a moment, he thought she might cry. Again. "You have no idea," she said, her voice tight.

"But I'd like to," he replied.

She opened her eyes. With careful deliberation, as if fearing she might faint again, she sat up. Hesitating, she slid off the table and took a seat on one of the rickety wooden chairs. Angel handed her the coffee. Her hands shook, and the hot liquid sloshed over the edges and onto her skin. She grimaced. "Hell, I keep doing that."

"Give it here—" Angel unwrapped her fingers from around the mug and took the ceramic container, handing it to Juan "—before you do some serious damage."

"I am not a child."

Angel nodded in acquiescence. "I don't think you are, but you've been through something traumatic." He pulled a chair closer and sat across from her, leaning with his elbows on his knees. "First, who are you?"

Her blue eyes widened. "Fiona. Fiona Macmillan."

"Tell me what happened, Fiona," Angel said.

"Tony and—" Her voice caught in her throat, and for a moment he thought she might break down. Instead, she continued, "Tony and I were at a hotel, the Luz del Bogotá."

Angel gave a short, curt nod. He knew the place. It had been a four-star hotel until a few years ago. Now, the stucco walls were pitted with bullet holes, and the only people who stayed there were lovers who couldn't afford better or the occasional *turistas* who were unfortunate enough to get a crappy travel agent.

She continued, "We were on the fourth floor, watching Montoya—"

"Ramon Montoya?" He tensed at the name. Montoya was not a man to cross, and as far as being a public servant…public enemy was closer to the truth.

She nodded. "Montoya was interrogating a woman, Maria Salvador. Do you know her?"

"Yes," Angel said. His gut tightened, not liking where this was going.

"What did he want?" Juan interrupted. Angel turned to see the bartender watching them, his hands twisted in a bar towel.

"He wanted names. People in the resistance. In RADEC," Fiona said. Her hands shook harder now. "He beat her."

"Is she—"

Fiona held up her hand, signaling silence. "Please let me finish," she said. Her eyes squeezed shut again, reminding Angel of a frightened child in a dark room, believing that if she opened her eyes, it would make the monsters real.

"We were watching Montoya and his men interrogate Maria. She refused to give up the names. To give that bastard anything. We thought he was letting her go. He told her to leave. Maria walked away.

"They shot her. Right there. Right in the courtyard. They shot her in the back." Fiona's voice broke, and for a heartbeat, the only sounds in the room were her sobs.

He wished there was something he could do to assuage her pain, but there was no fixing the situation. No bringing back the dead and reversing time. They had to move forward and act on the problems at hand.

"Maria's dead?" Juan whispered.

Fiona continued as if she hadn't heard him, her eyes still closed tight. "Tony jumped up and shouted. Montoya shot him, too. He died on the balcony in a pool of blood."

She opened her eyes. Liquid blue, they zeroed in on Angel. "The last thing he said was to find you."

Angel turned away from her stare, his fists tight. Tony was a good man, and he was dead by Montoya's hand. Both him and Maria.

Behind him, Juan broke into violent sobs.

A grip on Angel's arm caught his attention. Fiona's fingers squeezed, digging into the muscle. "So, here I am," she said, her calm, contained voice a sharp contrast to the tears of just seconds ago. "Can you help me?"

First things first, Angel reminded himself. Grief could wait. So could anger. "Did Montoya see you?"

She hesitated then shook her head. "I don't think so, but he knows someone was there. I heard his men talking. I won't have long until they put it all together."

Damn it.

"Juan." He grasped the sobbing man's shoulder. "I need you to check the perimeter. We need to know if she was followed. Can you do that?"

Juan nodded, wiped his eyes and left through the front door, shutting it firmly behind him.

Fiona watched Juan leave. "He loved her, didn't he?"

"He did."

"I'm so sorry," Fiona whispered.

"Me, too," Angel said. "But I need you to tell me what happened. Everything." Maybe there was something she'd forgotten. Something he could use to get her out of the mess she'd created.

"I've told you everything," Fiona said.

"Everything?" Angel asked. "I need more details."

"There is nothing else." Her eyes darted to the left and she reached up, twirling a strand of hair. "They died, and I ran until I walked through those doors."

Liar. He heard it in her voice and saw it in the physical tells she unconsciously displayed.

Of course, it was possible that whatever information she was hiding meant nothing of consequence. But he couldn't take that chance. His gut told him to get *all* the information. Most people ignored gut instinct. He wasn't one of them.

"You've left something out of your story." Elbows on the table, Angel templed his hands in front of his mouth. "In fact, when I think about it, you've left out quite a bit."

"Like what?" Fiona picked at a sliver of wood that stuck up from the table.

"Like *why*. Why were you two there? Spying for RADEC?"

"No. Nothing like that."

He didn't believe her. "Tony worked with RADEC, and you know it."

Fiona's hand stilled. "He was a member of RADEC?"

The surprise was real. She wasn't lying, at least not about that. Damn. But she was lying about something. "Fiona, I need you to talk to me. Tell me everything, or I can't help you."

Her gaze shot up. "There's nothing more to tell. Tony died. The last thing he told me was to come to you for help."

"Then he trusted me, and you'd do well to do the same. If you can't do that then leave. Now."

The fact that he meant it surprised him. He wasn't one to get involved, not anymore, but if he did, it sure as hell wasn't going to be under false pretenses.

Not even for Tony.

Fiona buried her head in her hands. "I'm sorry." When she looked up, she still appeared calm, but the guilt beneath the surface was almost tangible. "I was afraid if you knew, you might take the tape."

"Tape?" An unwelcome and unwanted déjà vu rippled up his spine.

"Yes. A tape. I'm a TV reporter," Fiona explained. "Tony and I were filming a story. Our big break." She laughed, but it was hollow and almost hysterical. "We got it, too. We recorded Maria's execution."

His hazel eyes wide, Angel stared at her. For a minute, Fiona wasn't sure if he was going to slap her or kiss her. "Tony died for a story?" he asked, though she didn't think it was a question but more of a private confirmation.

She waited.

"You're a reporter?"

Definitely a question this time. "I don't do local news.

Nothing like the weather, or traffic reports." He still seemed confused, suspicious and, if she wasn't imagining it, hurt.

"Well, I did," she said, continuing to explain, "but not anymore. I report on stories that matter." She realized how lame and trite the statement sounded and shut up before she said any more.

Too late, she realized as Angel's hazel eyes darkened. She'd hit a nerve. A big nerve. He looked *into* her. Fiona swallowed down the rising panic. "I take it that you have a problem with reporters?" she asked, dragging the question out.

"You take it right," Angel said. "Makes me wonder why Tony sent you here."

"Makes me wonder why you like Tony if you don't like reporters," Fiona shot back, hackles rising.

"I didn't know he was in the business," Angel said.

"I thought you were friends."

"We were," Angel said. "But even friends keep secrets."

Fiona straightened. That was an interesting comment.

"Besides, it's not *all* reporters. Just some of them," Angel said. His lips thinned, and Fiona braced herself for a verbal onslaught. "The ones that lack common sense and put themselves into danger, never thinking beyond the story. The ones that never consider that they might be killed, leaving others behind."

She didn't respond. Whoever Angel was ranting about, it wasn't her. Not anymore. But who? She wanted to ask but given the circumstances, prying into Angel's past seemed like a bad idea.

He continued. "What really pisses me off are the ones that get someone *else* killed."

Now they were talking about her. Fiona dropped her gaze to her hands, unable to meet Angel's hot gaze any longer. "I didn't think it would be dangerous," she said. "Not like that."

"Proving my point," Angel said.

He was upset. She understood that. But so was she. "If

you're trying to make me feel guilty, don't bother. I already feel responsible."

Angel hesitated then raked a hand through his hair. "Don't. It's not your fault."

Fiona shook her head. "I wish I could believe that." She didn't need to close her eyes to see Tony on the cold tiles, demanding she save herself even as he bled to death in front of her.

Angel reached over and took her hand, surprising her with his abrupt tenderness. "Tony knew what he was doing. My guess is that he wanted to catch Montoya doing something illegal. Something that would force the government to take action."

Fiona nodded. It made sense, and her head knew Angel was right. But her heart wasn't there yet. "Thanks."

He squeezed her fingers and held them tight. Fiona met his gaze. It was still hot. Still burned. But the heat was changing into something more.

Something that frightened her.

She yanked her hand from his. Shaking, she smoothed back her hair. "How did you know Tony? He must have trusted you a lot to send me here."

Angel clasped his hands on the tabletop. "He was a mercenary, once upon a time. We worked together on a few jobs."

"Tony, a mercenary? He couldn't have been," she said, incredulous. That was unbelievable.

"Why not?"

"Because mercenaries are just killers for…" Her voice faded as she realized what she was saying and who she was saying it to.

"Killers for hire?" Angel finished. "Cold-hearted bastards who would shoot their mothers for a buck?"

That was exactly what she'd thought. Heat bloomed on her cheeks. "No," she said. "It's just that he was a cameraman. A journalist."

"*And* a revolutionary *and* a mercenary," Angel finished.

"Tony killed people." It was hard to wrap her head around the thought. He was funny. Smart. Dedicated.

Or *had* been.

Angel was right—sometimes friends did have secrets.

"Yes. Sometimes. We did what we had to do. What we were paid to do," Angel said. "And some people need killing."

The matter-of-fact way he delivered the last sentence made her shiver. "I find that hard to believe," Fiona said.

"How about Montoya?" Angel challenged. "Do you think the fact that he's breathing makes the world a better place?"

She couldn't honestly say yes. "Point taken."

Angel took her hand again, his touch firm. Comforting. "If it makes you feel better, Tony didn't just kill people. He saved them. Hell, he saved me."

Now *that* sounded like Tony. "Is that why you're helping me?" she asked.

"One of the reasons," Angel replied.

Before she could ask about the others, the door opened and Juan came back in. His eyes were red. "No one is here, but it won't last," he said, his voice wavering.

"I'm a little obvious, aren't I?" she said, pulling a long blond strand of hair over her shoulder.

"Yes," Angel said. "And there are informants everywhere."

"So you'll help me?" Fiona said, latching on to hope for the first time since Tony died.

"You are sure Maria is dead?" Juan asked before Angel could reply.

She nodded. "Positive."

"Then we have no choice," he said.

Despite his impassioned words, the anguish in his eyes was unmistakable, and Fiona regretted the callous way she'd announced Maria's death. "I am so sorry," she said.

The bartender's brown eyes blackened as fury drowned

sorrow. "Her killers shall pay with suffering." He wiped his eyes with the heel of his hands and turned his attention to Angel. "I will have my revenge."

"No, *you* will not," Angel replied.

"You are saying that I cannot do this?" Juan stepped closer to Angel, daring him. Fiona tensed, not sure what she'd do if the two men came to blows. She might be able to stop Juan, but there was no chance of stopping Angel from doing anything he wanted.

"I'm saying that overzealousness will get you killed," Angel explained. "Training is what keeps men alive. Not passion."

"Then you help her," Juan snapped, jerking his head toward Fiona.

Angel rose. Fiona didn't miss the controlled way he stood, every move purposeful and directed. "I plan to. I owe Tony my life." He turned to Fiona. "What do you want?" he asked.

"I want to get this tape to my editor in the U.S."

He gave a slow nod and pulled his eyes away from the bartender. "Easy enough. I have a laptop in my room."

"Won't work," she said. "It's not digital."

"Not digital? Why?"

She blinked, remembering that she'd asked Tony the same question. Digital was so much easier, she'd argued. Faster. E-mailable. Instead of convincing Tony, her argument had sent him into a diatribe about how tape was classic. Richer. "He said tape was better."

"Tape?" Angel groaned. "What the hell was he thinking?"

"He said that if I wanted an award-winning story, I would need award-winning, quality footage."

"Sounds like Tony," Angel said. "Anal-retentive pain in the ass."

"Yeah, he was damned good." Her eyes watered as she realized she was talking about Tony in the past tense. "He wanted to make a difference. Wanted to break the story that put Montoya away. We didn't expect anyone to die."

"Please. Stop crying," Angel said, sounding desperate.

"Sorry," she said with a sharp laugh, noting the frantic edge to her voice. "It's been a bit of a Monday."

Once again, Angel wiped a tear from her cheek, and she tried not to sigh at the unexpected tenderness in his touch. She needed touch. Needed to feel safe. And for all his gruffness, Angel made her feel as if nothing bad could touch her again. "I need to get to a television studio," Fiona whispered. "They can transfer the footage to digital format, and then I can e-mail it to whoever we want."

"That won't keep you safe," Angel said. "Even if you send the story out, Montoya will come after you as long as you're in Colombia."

"Let's deal with the tape," she said. If she thought about the future beyond the tape, she'd start crying again. That, or go screaming down the street. "I want the world to see this man for what he is. Then we can discuss the next move."

Juan took her hand and squeezed her fingers. "Thank you for telling me about Maria," he said. "If we can put Montoya behind bars, she will not have died without purpose."

"You loved her, didn't you?"

He nodded, his eyes tearing again.

"If I could have saved her, I would have," Fiona said. "No one was supposed to die."

"It's not your fault. You are a brave woman."

"Brave?" Fiona laughed at the phrase. She wasn't brave. Numb was more like it.

"Yes," Juan said.

She didn't laugh again. Perhaps she didn't believe in herself as much as Juan did, but it didn't matter. She had the images of Tony's and Maria's deaths and the burning need to set things right to motivate her.

Courage meant little when compared to justice. "I'll get their story out," she vowed.

"Just finish Montoya," Juan said. "Make him pay for what he has done."

"I will," Fiona said. *For Tony. For Maria.*

"No, *we* will," Angel corrected.

"Thank you," Fiona said. Standing so close, he realized that darker circles, almost purple in color, ringed her blue eyes.

They were mesmerizing.

"Don't thank me yet," he said, reminding himself that her appearance was part of the job description and that pretty didn't equate with moral or good or smart. She was a reporter, and that meant she had more curiosity than common sense.

Just like Isabel.

Isabel. The woman he'd loved and buried. It was the millionth time he'd thought of her and the millionth time he pushed her memory away. Beautiful as Fiona, passionate as Maria, and a journalist in search of her big break, she'd died for her curiosity, leaving him behind to pick up the pieces of the past and bury the future.

What had Tony been thinking in sending Fiona—another Isabel in the making—to him when there were plenty of guns for hire in Bogotá? If the cameraman had lived, he'd be tempted to kill him himself. But Tony was dead and had left it to him to help Fiona. Angel scraped a hand through his hair, torn between the urge to shove the reporter out the door and live up to his duty by helping her.

"Ignore his temper," Juan said, changing the topic. "There is an independent television station just outside the El Parque de la 93 sector. They are friendly to RADEC and are eager to see Montoya stopped. Will that do?"

"Maybe," Fiona said.

"It'll have to do," Angel said. He needed to get this blond nuisance out of his hair as fast as possible. Unfortunately, El

Parque de la 93 was north of the city, which was hell and gone from where they were.

"Even though Juan didn't see anyone, we're going to assume you were followed, which means that we need to get you out of here. To someplace safe while I take the tape to the station."

Fiona's full lips turned downward. "*You're* taking the tape? I don't think so."

"I'm sure that since you're a TV reporter, you know that the El Parque de la 93 sector is dangerous," he said, not bothering to hide his derisive feelings regarding her profession.

She didn't appear to notice. "It's a wealthy area. Good shopping. Popular clubs—"

"Kidnappings," Angel interrupted.

"—and muggings," Fiona interrupted back. "I know all that. The wealth brings in more than the tourist trade."

Maybe she wasn't a total waste, Angel decided. She knew the region and its pitfalls, but book knowledge wasn't the same as street smarts. "There are also spies. People who would do anything for money. Including turning you over to Montoya." He rubbed the back of his neck with his hand. "You don't exactly blend."

"Ya think?"

He tried not to smile at her unexpected sarcasm.

"I can't let this tape out of my sight," she continued. "Tony trusted you, so I do, too. Kinda," she added with a slightly mocking half smile. "Besides, two people are better than one."

"Not when one is a tall blond reporter on the run," Angel countered.

Fiona took a step toward him, all defiance and determination. "I have the only tape. What if you're caught? I have to make sure this tape gets into the right hands."

Angel sighed in exasperation. He had two sisters and knew that tone. She wasn't going to back down, and there was no time to argue. He needed to get her to safety and get the footage to the public. And he was going to have to do it with her in tow. "Fine. But a few things first."

She relaxed, her shoulders dropping from their tense position. "Like what?"

"We wait until dark to head to the district."

"Isn't that when most robberies happen?"

"Yes, but Montoya won't expect you to travel then, and as for muggers, I can take care of them."

"No doubt," she said, her eyes traveling from his feet to his mouth. When she reached his eyes, her cheeks turned a bright red.

Angel chuckled. "Thanks for the vote of confidence."

Fiona gave a tentative smile, but her cheeks remained bright. "I just meant that since you're a mercenary, you can take care of yourself."

"I know what you meant," he said.

Juan squeezed her arm. "Angel is more than a mercenary. He is a hero. He will protect you."

Fiona nodded. "A hero? Who did you save?" she asked.

"He saved a busload of children from bandits," Juan said. "And another time, a village—"

"Shut up," Angel said. He didn't need the bartender telling Fiona his business.

"So, a bit more than a paid killer," Fiona said, her voice warm.

The thought of her admiring him, seeing him as a hero, rankled him. Admiration meant obligation, and he was up to his neck in responsibility. "No. I was paid. And I killed," Angel said. That was all she needed to know. Anything else was for friends, and Fiona was not on his *friends* list.

Her skin returned to its normal shade of pale, pink china. "Fair enough," Fiona said, the warmth gone from her voice. "I suppose I should pay you, then."

"Money's good," Angel said. He felt like an ass, but it was too late to back down now.

"So why help me?" she asked, staring at him with narrowed, curious eyes. "I can't pay you. Not yet."

"You can owe me."

"Agreed," she said. "Once the footage is safe, I'll get you your money. Somehow." Her eyes distant, she smiled for the first time. "And if this story wins an Emmy, I'll invite you to the party."

"An Emmy party?" Isabel had talked of the same thing the morning she left to get her big story.

He'd teased her about party aspirations as she'd walked out the door. Painful hindsight told him that he should have gone with her, but she hadn't told him the truth about the danger. If she had, he'd have kept her in bed. Safe in his arms.

Instead, she died for a story and a stupid award.

"Is winning the biggest prize all you people think about?" he asked, lashing out and not bothering to hide his contempt.

Fiona took a step back, her small smile fading. "I was making a joke. Kidding."

"There's truth in every joke," Angel said. "Who are you trying to fool? Me or yourself?"

Her cheeks turned pink again, and she returned his glare. "Forget I said anything," she said after a few seconds.

"Forgotten," he said, knowing it wasn't.

"Whatever," Fiona said, breathing so hard she trembled. "You know what? I don't need you, your mental baggage, or your attitude. I'll deal with this myself."

Despite her brave words, he didn't miss the fear and uncertainty beneath her anger. She couldn't do this alone, and they both knew it. "No. You won't," Angel said.

"Watch me," she said. Her eyes darkened, and she turned on her heel.

Angel sighed. Damn, she was determined to make him pay before she gave in to common sense. He watched her walk toward the door. He didn't think she'd actually try to solve her situation on her own, but when egos were involved it was hard to judge what someone might do.

Especially a reporter with a reputation at stake.

Still, if she wanted to play head games, he'd be happy to oblige. "I can't say that I'm surprised that you're a selfish pain in the ass," he commented when she was halfway across the room.

"Selfish?" She stopped midstep and turned to face him, her hands on her hips. "How can you say that?"

"You'd put the only evidence that we have against Montoya in danger because I'm not *nice* to you? Because I pissed you off?"

She bit her lower lip, thinking, and the unexpected urge to kiss her full, defiant mouth overwhelmed Angel. This was going to be harder than he thought, he realized. Much, much harder.

He followed her steps, not stopping until he was in her space. "We don't have to like each other to do this, do we?" he asked.

She tilted her head upward until her mouth was inches from his. The tension between them grew with each beat of Angel's heart. He crossed his arms over his chest, putting the barrier between them for both their sakes.

"I suppose not," she said.

"Good." Angel breathed a sigh of relief and stepped back.

"Yeah, good." She rocked back on her heels then forward again. "What now? We have hours to kill before nightfall. What do we do until then? Hide? Drink? Banter? Try not to kill each other?"

"We go to my apartment," Angel said. "And we go to bed."

Chapter 3

Fiona's jaw dropped as she stared at Angel, unable to believe he'd suggest sex after all she'd been through. She wanted comfort, but screwing a virtual stranger wasn't the path to solace. "I am not having sex with you," she squeaked.

He raised a brow. "I didn't say anything about sex. I said go to bed, and that's all I meant. We're going to have a long night ahead of us. We need to sleep when we can."

Once again, Fiona's cheek flushed with heat. Angel brought out the worst in her, and a part of her wished she had the option of walking away.

But she wasn't going anywhere. He might be irritating, and there were questions as to his sobriety, but Tony trusted him to protect her and that was enough.

Besides, there wasn't anyone else.

"Okay, sleep it is," she said. "Where to?"

"My place is a few buildings down."

"Fiona, here."

Fiona turned to see Juan toss her a bundle. She caught it in midair. She unrolled the cloth. There was an army-green floppy hat and a tan jacket. She put both on. The jacket reached past her thighs and helped hide the bloodstains. She tucked her hair inside the hat. "I'm ready," she said.

Angel assessed her from boot-clad feet to the top of her head. "It'll do," he said.

Like she had a choice.

"And this," Juan said, holding out a white bundle wrapped around a few clunky objects. "It's some bread and cheese," he explained. "A few bottles of water."

Fiona clung to the package, grateful for the gesture. It warmed her to know there were people out there who supported her. Who trusted her to do the right thing.

It was unfortunate that Angel thought so little of her, but she suspected it would take an act of God to convince him to trust her. She wished she knew why.

Fiona kissed Juan on the cheek. "Take care of yourself," she whispered in his ear.

"Don't worry about me." Juan said. "I'm closing up for a few weeks."

Fiona nodded. "Where will you go?"

He shrugged. "I am not sure. But there is little doubt that Montoya will track you here. It might be today. Perhaps tomorrow. Either way, I will not be here when he arrives."

Juan squeezed her hand. Hard. "And you need to go, as well," he said. "The longer you stay in the open, the greater the danger."

"He's right," Angel said.

Fiona nodded and broke away, following Angel out the door. The lock clicked after Juan shut the door behind them. She turned to see him glance out the window. She waved.

He flashed a small smile then put a sign in the window. *Cerrado.* Closed.

"Will he be okay?" she asked. She didn't know Juan, but she knew grief.

"He'll survive," Angel said, taking her arm and pulling her into motion. Fiona walked fast to stay by Angel's side as he led her down the sidewalk.

Though the street wasn't crowded, it wasn't empty, and Fiona lowered her head, trying not to call attention to herself.

"We're here," Angel said, stopping at the gate to his apartment building.

More like a condemned building, she thought when he opened the iron gate and let her in. Flaking yellow paint covered pitted stucco walls. The small courtyard was a riot of half-dead plants, and the dirt-filled fountain looked like it hadn't contained water in a decade. "Lovely," she said.

"It's a place to sleep," Angel replied. "And it's safe. Mostly."

That was all that mattered, she told herself. Keeping close, she followed Angel up three flights to a hallway lit with twenty-watt bulbs and smelling of burnt tortillas, sweat and mold. His door was the third down on the right. As he opened it, she dreaded what she'd find on the other side.

To her surprise, it was sparse but neat and smelled better than the hallway. She scooted inside and breathed a sigh of relief. "It's not horrible," she said.

"Gee. Thanks," Angel said, obviously not pleased with her comment.

Fiona scrubbed at her face, mentally kicking herself for being rude. What was it about Angel that gave her foot-in-mouth syndrome? "I'm sorry. That sounded ungrateful, and I'm not. You didn't have to do this, *any of this,* and I appreciate the chance you're taking in helping me."

"It's okay. We're both a little punchy." His expression softened, and he rubbed the back of his neck. "Just don't get too comfortable. We're not staying."

"Why not?" A shiver of goose bumps ran up Fiona's spine. "Were we followed?"

"No, but this is Bogotá. We're staying in another room. One that backs up to a fire escape."

"Won't the occupant notice?"

"No. It's mine. I rent it under another name."

He kept an extra room for escape? And she thought *she* was paranoid. "Why stay at all?" she asked. "If it's that dangerous, shouldn't we keep moving?"

"We will when it's dark," he explained. "Even with the hat, you stick out. So for now, we minimize risk, get rest, and hope we get lucky."

He went to the dresser, pulled out military-perfect, folded navy-blue T-shirts and black cargo pants. "Wearing those jeans is like wearing a bull's-eye," he said, handing her the clothes.

She held them up. The shirt reached midthigh, and the pants were a joke. "You don't think this will set me apart?"

"It'll do until we can get better," Angel said, pulling a gun from the dresser. Flat black in color, it looked lethal as hell.

Perfect.

"Change," he said, pulling another gun out. "I want to be out of here in sixty seconds."

He was serious. Dead serious. She ran into the small, dingy bathroom. The oversize shirt was manageable, but the pants were wide in the waist and pulled across her hips.

At least they'd stay on, she mused. After transferring the tape of Maria's death to one of the zippered cargo pockets, she pushed open the door as she tried to adjust the fit. "Got a—"

Fiona stopped midstep.

Angel stood with his back to her. With the exception of a pair of black boxers, he was naked. The muscles on his back flexed and moved. Every shadow perfect. Every line tight. But what caught her attention were the scars. A few were thin and white, as if made from a knife or a whip. Others were larger. Ugly.

He really was a mercenary, she realized. She'd known it before, but that was in her head. Now she knew—deep down knew—this man killed for a living. Or had.

Despite that, she longed to run her fingers over his battle scars. Test the texture of his skin and make the wicked lines disappear. To offer him the solace she craved.

Mesmerized, she stepped closer. A board squeaked beneath her feet. He glanced over his shoulder. "Do I have a what?" he asked without a hint of body consciousness as he slid a black T-shirt over his head.

"Belt?" she asked, tugging at the pants and staring at her feet. "Got a belt?"

"In the drawer." He grabbed a second set of black cargo pants and put them on, removing a few items from the pants on the floor and placing them in the various pockets. "Stuff your jeans and the other clothes under the covers."

She did as she instructed, making two long lumps side by side as she realized what he was trying to do. "That's not going to fool anyone," she said, shaking her head at the obvious decoy.

"It's not supposed to," Angel said. "If someone followed you, or if someone sells the info, Montoya will come in and shoot 'us' up." He sat on the bed and put on his boots. "Consider it an early warning system."

The goose bumps returned, and Fiona found herself speechless. A part of her mind wondered what she'd gotten herself into, but she knew the answer.

She'd crossed Ramon Montoya, and until she got the footage of Maria's death out of Colombia, her life was in danger.

Hers, and anyone she spoke to.

Juan.

"Will they come after Juan?" she asked, panicked at the thought. "If someone saw me go into the bar, they might."

Angel's hands stilled, and there was something new in his hazel eyes. Something she hadn't seen before and wasn't sure how to interpret.

Angel went back to lacing his boots. "He's already gone. He'll be fine." He finished and picked up his guns. "Take this," he said, holding one out.

It was for her? She eyed it. She'd shot a rifle before but only a few times. She took the gun. It was lighter than she expected.

"Can you shoot it if you have to?" he asked.

"Yes," she replied, hoping she sounded more confident than she felt. She put the weapon in a pocket then grabbed the small bag of food, the jacket and her hat.

Angel pressed a key into her hand. "End of the hallway. Last door on the left."

Slowly, he opened the door and edged into the hallway. "All clear. Go!"

The sun sank below the horizon, casting shadows and gold light over Fiona's sleeping body. She seemed much too innocent to be a reporter, Angel decided as he watched her sleep. She frowned, and her eyelids flickered, betraying the fact that she dreamed.

Bad dreams, he was sure.

He knew what those were like.

"Anthony," she mumbled, the dead man's name almost incoherent.

Yep, bad dreams. His back against the wall, a Glock on his lap and another tucked at the back of his waist, he touched a long, pale blond curl that had turned the color of honey in the setting sun.

Isabel's opposite, he mused. Isabel with her black hair, chocolate eyes and olive skin. He shut his eyes. Though it was over two years since her death, she still haunted him.

Fiona mumbled again. Whimpered. Kicked. Angel opened his eyes and stroked her hair, careful not to wake her. "Shhh," he whispered. "It's all right."

Her whimper turned into a sigh, and she turned over, sticking a leg out from the unzipped side of the sleeping bag.

She slept in her clothes in case they had to bug out, but even seeing her in boots and pants, he didn't miss the perfect curve of her thigh.

Looking at her, with her pale hair and a body that would make a monk question his vows, he knew he had nothing but trouble on his hands. Angel let his head fall back against the wall with a dull thud. When she'd asked for help, he should have told her to move on. To find someone else. But no, instead he had to play the hero.

Play being the operative word. He was a mercenary, dammit. Not a knight. And he would do well to remember that. He had a head full of memories to keep him in line. And if that wasn't enough, there was always Isabel's engagement ring to remind him about what happened to people who put themselves in situations better left alone. He touched the zippered pants pocket where he'd transferred it earlier.

"Crap, what a mistake," he muttered.

"What is?" Fiona turned over, blinking at him and yawning.

He stared at her, irked that she'd overheard his comment but more irked at himself for not keeping his mouth shut.

"Well?" she asked.

He ran a hand through his hair, not sure what to say other than the truth. "You. Me. Running from the law."

"I know, and I'm sorry."

She looked sorry. And helpless.

She sat up, crossing her legs beneath her. "If it makes a difference, I've thought about what you said earlier. About me putting people in danger for a story."

"And?" he asked, curious.

"I like to think that when it comes to humanity versus the story, I'd choose humanity. I'd save a life over getting a good story." Her voice trembled with uncertainty.

"You're not sure though, are you?" he asked, knowing that Isabel would have gone for the story every time. She couldn't help herself, even when it meant putting herself in danger.

Fiona shook her head. "In this case? No. Montoya needs to be stopped. That's not in question. Maria's death gave me the means to do just that. It isn't fair, but I'm glad I was there to capture it. And as for Tony…" Fiona ran her fingers through her hair. "I'll regret that for the rest of my life."

"Me, too," Angel said.

"But you need to know that despite what happened, I can't start questioning the morality of my job. What I can do is make sure that Montoya pays for his actions. That he goes to jail."

"I understand," he replied.

She managed a weak smile then stood, letting the sleeping bag drop to her feet, and went to the bathroom.

Angel watched her walk away from him, and his mouth went dry. He'd thought her legs were good. Her ass was better.

"I'll just be a minute," she said, closing the door.

Angel rose, asking himself again what he was doing. Then muffled sobs caught his ear. *Fiona.* She was sobbing in the bathroom, and not the fake crying that most women did. The kind that meant they wanted someone to comfort them but wanted the man to initiate the effort so they gave a half-hearted attempt to be quiet.

No. Her cries were almost silent. If the room hadn't been so quiet, he wouldn't have noticed.

It seemed she wasn't as emotionally distant from the day's events as either of them liked to pretend.

On the other side of the door, Fiona turned on the water, the splashing water covering the sound of her sobs.

Angel let his head fall back again. He should go in there. Comfort her. But what could he say? Tony and Maria were dead, and nothing he said or did would change the past.

"This is what I meant by mistake," he said to no one. Everything she did, everything she was, made her a distraction. The water stopped, and silence reigned again.

Angel rose, stretching, and peeked out the front window. People going to and from the market filled the streets along with cars that were comprised more of rust than metal. Children played. Men stood in groups, smoking cheap cigarettes and talking to each other.

No one glanced his way or did anything that appeared the least suspicious, but that meant nothing. Any one of them would sell Fiona out. They were poor and putting food on the table took precedence over a *gringa* with a supposed tape of Montoya killing a rebel leader.

The sound of gunshots reverberated in the room.

Montoya. They'd found the dummies. Damn, he'd hoped they'd have more time. It was at least thirty minutes until dark.

"It's him!" Fiona barreled out of the bathroom, running into Angel.

"I know," he said, taking a deep breath and controlling the sudden rush of adrenaline that surged through his blood. They had thirty seconds. Maybe.

There were shouts, and then the sound of doors splintering as Montoya's men made their way down the hallway, checking the rooms.

Angel ran to the window that faced the alley and the fire escape. The window slid up on well-oiled tracks. He might not live in the room but he made sure he maintained it since there was no point in having an escape route that was ineffective.

"Climb up." He stood aside, his weapon trained on the door.

To her credit, Fiona didn't argue but clambered out onto the rickety metal steps and headed toward the roof.

Angel followed, sliding the window shut. Not that their escape would fool the thugs for long, but if he and Fiona made the roof before they arrived, the men might assume they'd gone down.

It was what most people would do.

Above him, Fiona climbed onto the roof, her booted feet disappearing over the edge. In the room below, he heard the door splinter. He pushed himself and in seconds joined Fiona on the roof.

The sound of breaking glass followed. In the dimming light, Fiona's eyes widened. "What do we do?" she asked, her voice low and shaky.

"We jump."

"Excuse me?"

There was no time to explain. Grabbing her arm, he hurried her to the far side of the building. The next building was five feet away. "Jump to the next roof."

She leaned over the edge. "That's a helluva drop."

"Would you prefer a bullet?"

She paled but shook her head, walked back a few feet and barreled toward the edge. It's just five feet, he told himself as she launched herself into the air and over the alley. She landed on the other side, feet solid on the flat, tarred surface. Facing him, she motioned for him to hurry.

Good girl.

He leapt and landed next to her. "Again," he said, gesturing toward the next building.

"If they come up here, we'll be sitting ducks on these flat roofs," Fiona said.

"I know. So quit talking and get moving. Get to the next building, then we go down on the far side."

She frowned but ran, clearing the five-foot span with ease, and headed across the roof without a glance back.

He hurried, not breaking stride and staying on her heels. They reached the ladder as a gunshot rent the air, ripping into the graveled tar paper a few inches from Angel's feet. Fiona froze.

The goons were smarter than he thought, and he had the suspicion that in better light, they'd have hit him. "Hurry!" he shouted.

Fiona slid down the ladder, using her feet and hands on the outside edges to push inward on the rails and create a controlled fall.

Gravel peppered his legs, and Angel turned, firing back. There was a cry, and in the growing shadows, one of the men fell to the ground.

He hoped it hurt. A lot. Sticking his gun into the back of his pants, he slid down the ladder, as well, dropping the last few feet.

"What do we do?" Fiona asked, already edging toward the entrance to the alley and the crowds that offered some protective anonymity.

"We walk," Angel said. Taking her arm, he pulled her close, and they entered the crowd. It took less than thirty seconds to realize his mistake. Fiona was close to six feet tall, making her stand out. Where was her hat? Her blond hair stood out like a beacon.

Men were already turning heads, gawking at her. They wouldn't proposition her since she had him as an escort, but if Montoya's men questioned anyone, there would be no doubt that they'd remember the exotic blonde.

Damn it. He walked faster

"What are you doing? Slow down."

"You're too damned pretty. I knew it would be a problem," Angel muttered.

"Well, excuse me," Fiona whispered. "It's not like I do it on purpose. You want to complain? Take it up with my parents for giving me the good genes."

He glanced at her, too worried and focused to give her points for being right. "We've got to cover your head," he said. Entering the outdoor market, he worked his way in through the crowds.

"Wait here," he said, leaving Fiona in front of a booth crammed with spices and dried fruit.

"Wait?" Her eyes were dark in the dim lights, but her pale skin glowed. "Where are you going?"

"I need to buy a few things, and I do not want anyone to remember that I bought them for you."

"Are you coming back?" she asked, clutching at his arm.

Under any other circumstances, he'd be insulted at the insinuation he would abandon someone under his protection, but the fear in her voice negated any insult. He gripped her shoulders and met her uneasy stare. "I am coming back. I promise."

She swallowed and gave him a tight nod. "Okay. Just hurry."

Almost running, Angel stopped at the first booth that sold clothes. There was no time for haggling. He grabbed a red shawl and a hat, pressing pesos into the vendor's hand.

"That was more than thirty seconds," Fiona said, as she took the garments, gripping them like a lifeline.

"So sue me," Angel said.

She put on the large hat, stuffing her hair inside, and wrapped the shawl around her, hunching over. "How's this?" she asked.

The disguise wasn't great. Nothing short of hair dye and a sudden drop in height would make her blend in with the locals.

Behind him, there were shouts. Montoya's men. They couldn't be far behind.

Taking her hand, he pulled her back into the throng of people. "Good enough."

Chapter 4

Angel looked over Fiona's shoulder as she gazed at herself in the motel room's cracked bathroom mirror, glanced at the box and then back at herself. She held up a box of hair color, drawing his attention from her expressive eyes. "They didn't have brown? I'll look like a Goth wannabe."

Angel chuckled at the image in his head.

"It'll look hideous," she hissed.

The thought of being less than beautiful probably wasn't something she was used to, but remorse was the farthest thing from Angel's heart. "There were only three options." He ticked them off on his fingers. "Black. Red. Blonde."

"I don't know…"

"I only rented the room for two hours. Let's get this done and get out of here while it's still early," Angel said, biting back his irritation. It was just hair, for crying out loud. It wasn't as if he were asking her to shave her head or turn herself orange with a cheap self-tanner.

She glared at him. "Fine."

He held back the urge to roll his eyes. He knew that when a woman said *fine,* there was thirty minutes' worth of subtext beneath the single word, but that didn't mean he was going to ask her about it.

He didn't care that much, he told himself. This was a favor for a dead man. A job. Helping *her* because he was the kind of man who kept his word. *Nothing more.* "Good. Take off your shirt."

Her eyes widened. "Excuse me?"

"Our resources are limited. Unless you want to run around smelling like a cheap beauty parlor, I suggest you remove it. Now."

She didn't seem convinced, and in fact, stared at him like he was a pervert.

"Don't flatter yourself," he said, replying to her unfriendly stare with a dare. "I've seen it all before. I wouldn't care if you were naked."

Still facing the mirror, her rigid stance told him she was determined to match him in the stubborn department.

He didn't back down, though he knew that if Fiona asked and if he were truthful, he'd admit that he did care. Very much.

Her eyes narrowed, and in a single move, she pulled her shirt over her head and stood in the middle of the stale, dingy bathroom in nothing but a pink bra and his black pants.

The cramped room felt suddenly devoid of air. He hadn't expected her to take his challenge and remove the garment while he was in the room.

Now that she had, there was only word for Fiona. *Perfection.* The thought caught him unaware. Angel turned on his heel. "I'll let you get to it."

"I thought you didn't care," Fiona said.

He stopped midstep.

She rattled the box. "Unless you want me to be even more obvious, I'll need you to help with the back of my head to make sure I don't miss any spots."

He hesitated, sure she was baiting him on purpose but unable to argue with her logic and even less willing to walk away from the unspoken dare since she'd called him on his. He turned back. "Give it over." She handed him the box, and he tried to ignore her as she combed her pale hair out with the cheap brush he'd purchased.

God help him, he wanted to run his hands through the strands. See if they were as silky as they appeared. Instead, he opened the box and let the various tubes and bottle roll into the sink.

Pulling out a piece of paper, he opened it to find a pair of gloves folded inside. He set them on top of the bottles and read.

"Reading the directions?" Fiona smiled. "There's a first. If the *man union* finds out, you might get expelled."

He ignored the gibe. It seemed like a straightforward process. Mix the B tube with the ingredients of A and apply.

He picked up the gloves. "Crap."

Fiona's eyes slid from his hands to the tiny pieces of plastic that appeared two sizes too small. "Maybe I should do this."

"Have you ever colored your hair?"

She let a swatch of blond slide through her fingers. "Nope. This is all me."

All over? He managed to keep the words in his head. "I'll do it," he said. "As you pointed out, we don't want any missed spots."

"It's your skin." She took a deep breath, and it took every ounce of control to keep his eyes from sliding to her breasts.

Her perfect, lace-bound breasts.

"Sit." The command came out harsher than he intended, but she didn't argue, or even balk, as she flipped down the toilet lid and sat.

"I hate this," she said, all defiance and boldness gone from her blue eyes.

"I know." Angel almost felt sorry for her. Was she more than her blond hair, flawless skin and perfect breasts?

They were about to find out.

He picked up the plastic bottle and shook it, mixing the contents. Shoving his hands into the thin gloves, he squeezed the dark color down the part in her hair. Carefully, he worked the contents through the blond strands, fighting off the urge to glance downward at her porcelain flesh.

For a few awkward minutes, there was nothing but the sound of their breathing echoing on the tile and, even with the door open, the acrid, hair-coloring chemicals making both cough. "Done." He sighed in relief, sliding off the tight gloves and tossing them into the sink.

Fiona rose, looked at herself in the mirror, and frowned. "This is going to be a disaster."

"Probably," Angel agreed.

She raised a brow, and he groaned. "We forgot your eyebrows."

"Oh hell." Turning to face him, she shut her eyes, and her mouth turned downward at the corners. "Just do it and please, be careful. I don't want to look like Groucho Marx when we're done."

She was close enough for him to feel her breath against his skin. Using his pinky, he transferred a small bit of the black hair color to her eyebrows, being careful to leave her surrounding skin as stain free as possible. "Don't open your eyes," he said. "The fumes could strip the paint off a wall."

"What am I supposed to do?" Her eyes squeezed shut, and her nose wrinkled at the obnoxious smell. "Just stand here?"

"Here." He took her hand to help her sit down. Her skin was smooth, soft, and for a flicker of insanity, he wondered how her fingers would feel on his bare skin. When she was perched on the toilet lid again, he let her hand slide from his with a shudder of relief.

"Thanks," she said, managing to appear both bored and—

despite the chemical giving her hair a matted, quasi dreadlocked appearance—beautiful.

He knew it verged on voyeurism, but he took the opportunity to stare at her half-naked body. She really was perfect. Not a bit of silicon or surgery.

Just natural beauty.

Perfect for a reporter, he told himself, turning away. Her long hair, stunning eyes and perfect breasts would probably land her a spot on prime-time television one day.

Isabel would have envied her opportunities.

"Quit staring at me," Fiona said.

"I'm not," he replied.

"Liar," Fiona said with a smirk. "You might not like me but you're still a man. All men are a bit voyeuristic. It's genetically encoded into their biological makeup."

Angel snorted in disbelief. "Think you know men that well?"

She nodded. "I'm pretty, not dumb."

"The jury is still out on that," he shot back.

She stiffened, and he knew he'd hit a nerve, no matter how unintentional. "Gee, thanks." Her mouth curled into a perfect, ruby-colored sneer. "I didn't know you were part of the 'she's pretty so she must have the IQ of a rock' club."

Angel hesitated. She had a point. A good one. There was nothing more irritating than being judged based on one aspect of self—like being a mercenary—and there was nothing more shallow than being the person doing the judging.

But he refused to feel bad, and he sure as hell wasn't going to apologize for a simple, stupid off-the-cuff comment. "What I'm saying is that you lack gut instinct," he tried to explain.

"About men? I don't think so."

"About life," he countered. "Which has nothing to do with your IQ and everything to do with the fact that you're inexperienced and in over your head."

"Says who?"

"Says Tony."

"Oh." Fiona took a deep breath. Though she kept her eyes shut, a shimmer of tears glimmered on the fringes.

Angel scrubbed his face with his palms, glad her eyes were closed because he knew he'd acted like a jerk. "Let's rinse your eyebrows off," he said, changing the topic. "We don't want you to go blind."

Waiting for the hair color to do its work, Fiona sat alone in the bathroom, avoiding the mirror and listening to Angel's heavy footsteps pace the length of the small bedroom just beyond her. She wanted to dislike Angel. Hate him. Anything besides agree with him.

But his comments, even the small ones, haunted her now that she had time to think.

Especially the ones about her being too pretty and that it would cause him trouble. He didn't know it, but her appearance was one of the reasons Tony had died.

To her, the fact she was beautiful was simply luck of the draw. Sure, she used it to her advantage, and flirting had saved her from more than one speeding ticket, but big blue eyes and blond hair didn't always help her.

To some women, she was a threat. To men, something pretty to put on their arm. Worse, to her network, her looks translated into a lack of connection with the audience. Viewers watched her but couldn't associate with her. Didn't believe she could understand, or report, their problems with genuine empathy.

As if being pretty left her with no worries of her own.

She shook her head. "I wish."

So, instead of being given prime stories, her boss tagged her as "pretty but stupid" and gave her stories that dealt more with supermodels and less with the world at large.

Tony had been one of the few men who never tried to get her into bed and, even more amazing, saw past the pretty face.

She wished the station saw her through his eyes.

Then Tony made a proposal she couldn't refuse. They would both take time off, but instead of a vacation, they'd go to his native Colombia and find a story worthy of reporting. Something that would make their careers and help Tony's people. True, it was unorthodox, but Tony pointed out that if they waited for the network to give them a prize-winning story, they'd be too old to enjoy the moment. They had to seize it themselves. Now.

Fiona had jumped at the chance to go to Colombia with her cameraman. And it was also why, when it came down to it, he'd died. Because she wanted to be more than a pretty face.

Angel had been right about the consequences of her inexperience, but she already knew that and being reminded wasn't necessary. Whenever she closed her eyes, she saw blood. Everywhere.

No, she really didn't need a reminder. Her chest tightened, and she took a deep breath.

"Time's up," Angel said, knocking on the door a split second before coming into the bathroom.

She released her breath, letting it take the tension and guilt with it.

"Okay," she said. It was time to see the damage. She gritted her teeth and reached for the gloves, but Angel stopped her with a firm hand.

"There's no way you'll get that mess rinsed by yourself." Taking the gloves, he slipped them on and, since there wasn't a tub in the room, turned on the water in the sink. "Bend over."

Shutting her eyes, she bent over the chipped porcelain basin, grateful for the few additional minutes of reality avoidance. Angel buried his hands in her hair and carefully guided her head down into the water.

With unexpected gentleness, he rinsed her hair, starting at her scalp and working his way through the long strands. Even with gloves, the heat of his hands penetrated her skin, and she fought the urge to lean into his touch. When was the last time a man had touched her?

She searched through memory and realized the last time a man made her feel that wonderful, hot sensation in the pit of her stomach was over two years ago. She'd put her entire life on hold for her career and that included any semblance of a sex life.

Now, of all times, her hormones chose to rage to life? With Angel? She blamed adrenaline, the desire to run from her guilt and her recent monastic state.

Great.

"Is that okay?" Angel asked, his hands returning to her scalp as the warm water trickled over her hair. "Too hot?"

She was flushed. Her heart raced. And she was sure her knees would buckle given half a chance.

She counted it a blessing that he couldn't see her face. She swallowed hard. "It's fine," she replied. Adjusting her stance, she grazed him with her bottom. He froze.

"Good." The single word sounded like a strangled groan. He continued rinsing her hair. She wondered if he was as uncomfortable as her.

She hoped so. She hated to suffer alone.

Trying not to smile at the thought, Fiona focused on the water running over her head, letting the sound fill her ears. Angel's touch strengthened. He stroked her scalp and the sides of her neck, working the color from her hair.

Her smile died as her desire ratcheted up a notch, and she imagined what his hands would feel like on the rest of her body. Gentle but firm. Tender but with the strength of a man who knew what he wanted and how to get it.

If only he wanted her…

Stop it, Fiona, she told herself and steeled herself against his touch and her inappropriate libido.

Just when she thought she might crack, the water stopped, and Angel squeezed the excess water from her hair. He covered her head with a thin towel and pulled her upright.

Moment of truth. She opened her eyes.

The towel hid her hair, but her eyebrows and skin were in plain view. Lust for Angel died, replaced with horror at her appearance. She clamped her hands over her mouth and stifled a groan. Despite Angel's best efforts, black dye stained the skin around her eyebrows and around the edges of her face. She wished she could accuse him of doing a half-assed job on purpose but knew it wasn't true. He was a professional. He needed her to appear as inconspicuous as possible.

This was not inconspicuous.

He frowned. "I'm sure it'll come off." Pushing her aside, he applied a sliver of soap to a square of cloth that served as a washrag and turned her to face him. "Hold still and shut your eyes," he said. Grasping her chin, he scrubbed at her right eyebrow.

It wasn't gentle or sensuous—it was closer to being attacked with a Brillo pad. Fiona winced.

"Hold still," Angel said. His grip tightened.

"Is it coming off?"

"Yes." He attacked her other brow, and she braced herself against the sink.

He moved to her hairline, and she gritted her teeth, sure he was stripping away multiple layers of epidermis. This is for your own benefit, she reminded herself. To keep you safe. To make Tony's death mean something.

The scrubbing stopped. "Oh, thank God," she sighed in relief, the words slipping out before her she could stop them.

Angel chuckled in reply.

She opened her eyes, rolling them at him before she glanced

back into the mirror. Her skin was red and raw, but the staining was almost nonexistent. "Better," she said.

"How about the hair?" he asked, moving to tug the towel off her head.

She stopped him. "I'll finish up in here," she said, wanting him gone before she unveiled the disaster that was once her trademark.

His eyes softened. "I'll be outside."

She turned back to her reflection, unable to bear his pity. It was easier to ignore him when he acted like a chauvinistic jerk and treated her like a self-obsessed moron. That Angel she expected.

The kind one confused her.

He shut the door behind him, leaving her alone. Fiona held her breath, counted to three, and pulled the towel off her hair.

Her once-beautiful blond hair hung in lanky strands. Ratty. Thick, twisted and so black it had blue highlights. "Oh, that's subtle," she said, tears welling in her eyes even as she picked up the brush and got to work.

Angel sat on the bed, waiting for the screams. Wails. Something besides the silence.

The silence creeped him out.

He lasted another fifteen minutes before he called out, "Are you all right?"

In response, the door squeaked opened, but Fiona stayed on the other side. "You're not going to like it," she said.

Him? "I'm sure it'll be fine," he said, smirking despite a self-promise to refrain from giving her a bad time about her hair.

The door opened all the way, and Fiona stepped into the room with an uncertainty he was sure was foreign to her.

Jet-black hair fell in damp waves over her shoulders, framing her face and making her blue eye bluer. Striking. Despite his intentions, he'd managed to make her prettier. "Oh, hell," Angel groaned, resting his head in his hands.

"Told you," Fiona said.

Hands templed against his mouth, he shook his head. "Can't you even *try* to blend? To look average?"

Her brows rose, and she shrugged. "We've had this conversation. Genetics. Parents. Not. My. Fault."

"But this," he gestured toward her hair. "How did you manage to make it *hot?* It's an obnoxious color—or I thought it was until now."

"Did you want me ugly or did you want me to not look like me?" she asked. "I thought the latter was more important, and call me crazy, but this doesn't look like me anymore. Not really."

She made a good point. She was still beautiful, but the dark hair, pale skin, and blue eyes gave her an exotic appearance. Most people would subconsciously explain that away. There were few people in Colombia who could claim to be indigenous. Hell, his Spanish ancestry gave him a height and build that was uncommon for this region and no one gave him a second glance.

It's the skin, he decided. Pale skin. Black hair. It was a lethal combination. Perhaps he'd buy her some self-tanner. He hadn't seen any in the store, but a bigger store might have some.

He took a longer look at her and realized it wouldn't matter. Tanned. Fair. Blond hair. Black. None of it mattered. Fiona couldn't help but be beautiful.

What a pain.

A pounding on the door made Fiona jump. Angel's hand went to the gun on his hip. *"¿Quién es él?"* he called out. No one knew they were here.

"Si usted desea quedarse, usted tiene que pagar," a male voice answered.

The manager wanted more money. Had two hours passed already? Angel didn't mind the additional pesos, but he sure as hell wasn't going to open the door with a brand-new Fiona standing in the room.

"What do we do?" Fiona asked, blue eyes wide.

"Get in the bathroom."

She opened her mouth to ask or argue—he didn't care which—but his narrowed eyes and tight mouth told her to shut up louder than any words.

She snapped her mouth closed and went into the bathroom.

Angel pulled out a few pesos and opened the door. He didn't recognize the man as the one he'd paid earlier. Maybe he was legit. Maybe not. Either way, Angel had to act as if all was right with the world. Wordless, he pressed the bills into the man's sweaty palm.

The man tried to look past him, but Angel blocked his view. *"Salga,"* he said. *Get out.*

All he received in return was a grunt as the man turned and left. *"Una hora,"* he called out over his shoulder.

One hour.

Angel slammed the door shut, and Fiona came out of the bathroom. "What happened?"

He removed a pillowcase and tossed it to Fiona.

She snatched it in midair with a worried expression. "What's wrong?"

"Maybe nothing," Angel replied. "You have five minutes."

"I'll get our things—"

"No. Clean the bathroom," Angel interrupted. Yanking the thin cover off the bed, he handed it to Fiona. "I don't want the owner coming up and discovering we changed your hair. The less he knows, the less Montoya can find out."

"You think Montoya will find out we were here?"

"I think he has enough power and money to do whatever he wants," Angel replied. "Make sure the sink is clean then put everything in the pillowcase. We'll take it with us and toss it later."

She got to work with no argument while Angel went over the room, making sure they hadn't left any clues that pointed to them or where they were going.

Not that it mattered. What he'd said about Montoya was true. It wasn't a matter of *if* Montoya found their trail; it was a matter of *when*. Even dyeing Fiona's hair was simply a temporary solution to the problem of Montoya and his goons.

"Done." She came out with pillowcase in hand.

He opened the window, and she slid over the ledge and dropped into the dark alley behind the motel without question. Taking one last look to make sure they hadn't left anything behind, Angel followed, unable to shake the feeling that something was going to go wrong and soon.

Chapter 5

Drinking coffee at a small café, Angel and Fiona sat across from the television station Juan had suggested. The brick building was closed, but it was early. Too early, as far as Angel was concerned, and a long morning was made longer by a night on the run.

He sipped his coffee, caffeinating himself, and hoped that today went better than yesterday. If so, he'd have Fiona on a plane back to the States by sunset, and he could go back to his life.

His life. It wasn't much and hadn't been for a long time, but he knew one thing in the plus column—it was bullet free.

"You okay?" Fiona asked.

Angel glanced across the street. There was movement in the windows. He hadn't seen anyone enter through the front, which meant there was a back door.

Excellent.

"I'm good. Why?" Angel asked, signaling for the check.

"You seemed a little off for a minute." She peeked at him over the rim of the cheap, dark sunglasses, which they'd purchased last night from a sidewalk vendor, as if expecting a reply.

He shrugged. She could expect all day. He wasn't going to tell her anything. Setting a few pesos on the table, he rose. "Let's do this."

She frowned in what he thought might be disappointment, then her mouth flattened, and she tilted her head up until the black lenses hid her eyes once again. They rose and crossed the street. "Think it's safe?" Fiona asked as they dodged a car that seemed hell-bent on making a light before it turned red.

"I think so," Angel replied. They weren't followed, he was sure of that. However, he held no illusions that safety was anything but fleeting. Montoya was searching for both of them. It was only a combination of Angel's skill and good luck that had kept them alive so far.

And the latter might abandon him at any moment.

Hurrying, Angel pushed open the door of the station, standing aside to let Fiona enter.

A bored receptionist, hair piled high on her head and wearing too much makeup for someone who barely qualified as an adult, sat behind a cheap desk. "Good morning," Angel said. "I'd like to speak to whoever's in charge."

She didn't bother to look up from her fashion magazine. "He's not here."

"Then anyone will do."

She thumbed the page over, not bothering to reply.

Reaching over, Angel took the magazine from her grasp, closed it, and set it back on the desk. "Please. Now."

For a long moment, the receptionist stared at the couple. Did she recognize them? Next to him, Fiona held her breath. Finally, with a dramatic sigh the receptionist picked up the phone and punched in an extension with a long, manicured nail. "Carlos, there's someone here to see you." There was a pause.

She was oblivious to their identities.

"What do you want?" the girl asked Angel, not bothering to put her hand over the receiver.

"Tell him we have a tape that might be of interest to him."

"Of what?"

Angel shook his head. "He's either interested or not. We can go elsewhere if he's not."

The girl repeated the information then hung up the phone with an irritated sigh. "Go on back," she said, reaching under the desk. There was a buzz then the click of a door being unlocked.

So the office wasn't as low-tech as it appeared. That was good but didn't mean he could relax. There would be no relaxing until Montoya was stopped.

Angel led the way down the dim hallway and into the studio, prepared for an ambush and praying he was wrong.

A total of five men prepped the room. None seemed interested in either him or Fiona. Still, Angel didn't trust them. Keeping to the edge of the room, he inventoried the interior. Televisions, cameras and multiple boards with myriad lights, switches and buttons were crammed into the small space. A few doors lined the walls, and he made note of the one that led to the alley.

Probably where employees entered to come to work, since he hadn't seen anyone go through the front door, he decided.

One of the many doors opened, and Angel tensed. An older man, his clothes wrinkled, with bags under his eyes and a scowl on his mouth, came toward them, his expression a combination of interest and irritation.

When he was within a few feet, he stopped. His eyes widened.

Angel knew that look. Recognition. Dammit, they were made.

He had known his luck wouldn't last, but he'd hoped for a few more hours. Calmly, he turned Fiona around midstep and pointed her back toward the exit.

"Wait," the older man called out.

With his free hand, Angel reached for the weapon concealed under his shirt.

The cadence of footsteps quickened. Angel increased his pace, keeping Fiona close to his side.

In seconds, the man reached them. "Please," he said, matching his pace with Angel's long strides. "I know who you are. I want to help."

Fiona slowed, forcing Angel to follow suit. "What are you doing?" he growled. "Get moving. Now."

"No," Fiona said, keeping her voice low. "We came here for help, and he's offering."

"He knows who we are," Angel argued. Didn't she have any preservation instincts? At all?

"I get that," Fiona countered, her hand gripping his arm. "But that means there's something else going on. Something we don't know about. We should find out what that something is before we go back out there."

Angel hesitated. As much as he hated to admit it, she made a good point. He stopped, turning to their pursuer. "You want to help? How?"

The old man smiled. "Come with me."

Angel didn't want to go anywhere besides out the front door, but between Fiona's grip and the old man's insistence, he knew he was beaten. And if there was a problem, he was armed. "Just hurry."

Quickly, the old man led them into a small room that contained a small cot and a table and smelled like stale coffee. A single barred window let in the morning sun, and another door led to God knew where. With the exception of the disheveled man, there was no one else.

Shutting the door behind them, Angel pulled his gun. The man paled. Angel didn't care. "How do you know us?"

"It's not just me. Your face is all over the television."

"Damn it," Angel swore. The situation was worse than he thought.

The man turned to Fiona, squinting. Then he smiled. "My name is Carlos Rios. Miss Macmillan, you are just as beautiful with black hair." He took her hand in his, kissing the pale skin with unexpected charm. Heat rushed through Angel's blood. Primal. Forceful. And it screamed, Mine.

But she wasn't. Not really. She was his to protect, he reminded himself, and that wasn't by choice but by obligation.

"Would you care to explain?" Angel said, his words polite but his tone anything but courteous.

"Your pictures are plastered everywhere. They say you," he gestured toward Angel, "murdered Maria Salvador and a cameraman. There is a citywide manhunt for you and your American accomplice."

"We're not killers." Fiona shook her head, raking a hand through her hair in distress. "I'm a reporter!"

"Calm down," Angel said. "We don't need anyone running in here."

"Calm down?" Fiona asked, her body shaking with anger. "We're not killers. How can anyone think that?"

"No, you're not a killer, but I am," Angel reminded her.

Fiona hesitated. "You've killed, but you didn't kill Maria or Tony. Besides, you might have killed but you're not a murderer. There's a difference."

There was a difference, but it was a surprise to hear she understood it. Yes, he had killed. But it was to protect others. Never out of anger. Never for passion.

And never for power.

"It gets worse," Carlos said, interrupting them before Angel could respond.

"Tell me," Angel said, focusing his attention on the issue at hand.

"They are offering a reward. Ten thousand dollars American."

Angel groaned at hearing the amount. They were screwed. No, they were worse than screwed. They were dead unless they got out of Bogotá.

Hell, unless they got out of Colombia. "Time to go," he said.

"Wait," Carlos said.

"Why?" The longer they stayed in one spot the more likely they'd be discovered.

"You're here for a reason. What is it?"

"The tape your receptionist mentioned. It shows who killed Maria," Fiona said before Angel could stop her or reply. "And it wasn't me or Angel."

Angel didn't miss the glint in Carlos's eye. He'd seen it before in both Isabel and Fiona and it had nothing to do with reward. The man was thinking about the potential for worldwide recognition for his tiny station.

"You have this tape in your possession?" Carlos asked.

"Yes," Fiona replied, oblivious to the danger of her continuing revelations.

Angel bit his tongue. This was exactly what he meant when he told Fiona she had no life experience. For a reporter, she lacked slyness.

And while her candor might be endearing in normal life, now was not the time. Still, the cat was out of the bag and there was no putting it back. Instead, Angel did what he was trained to do— watch, learn as much as possible and then use that information to his advantage.

Fiona continued. "I need to transfer the tape to digital so I can e-mail it to my editor. Can you help me?"

"This is big. Maria was a member of RADEC," Carlos mumbled. Finally, he gave a slow nod. "You will give me credit. A byline."

Fiona's blue eyes darkened, and Angel watched her reaction

with interest. Would she agree to share the accolades, or would they spend the afternoon looking for another station and dodging wannabe bounty hunters?

She bit her lower lip. "This is my story. People died to get it," she said.

"This is my station," Carlos countered. "Everything that leaves it has my stamp on it. You are welcome to go elsewhere if you do not like the terms."

Nice old man, my ass. Angel frowned. Next to him, Fiona's breathing grew rapid. "Fine," she replied through clenched lips. "It's not like we have much choice."

Angel cocked his head in surprise. He hadn't expected her to agree at all, much less with such little persuasion.

"But you'll have to help us," Fiona said. "Get us out of here and to safety."

Angel grinned, pleased to see there were brains beneath the beauty and that she wasn't giving up the tape without getting something in return. She didn't have his street smarts, but she wasn't dumb. Not when their lives were on the line.

Carlos hesitated then held out his hand. "Deal."

She took it, giving it a firm shake. "Let's get to work."

Angel exhaled his tension. A little computer magic and he'd be on his way back to Tierra Roja by noon and downing a shot of mescal. Well, maybe not Tierra Roja. It would be a long time before Juan's bar—and Bogotá in general—was safe for him. But he'd find some place, somewhere.

He glanced at Fiona. She was still pissed. Her skin flushed, making her blue eyes appear brighter. Arms crossed over her chest, she tossed her head, sending her black hair flying.

And somehow, the prospect of finding a bar didn't seem as pleasant as it had a second ago.

"I'll send the crew away, and we'll get started," Carlos said. "Wait here." He opened the door. There was a popping sound, and the man fell to the floor, screaming and holding a hand over his bloody thigh.

Gunfire. Adrenaline flooded Angel's body. Years of training and experience took over. He breathed deep, brought the unexpected strength to heel.

Fiona screamed. Already moving, he gave her panic no more than a cursory thought. Instead, he dropped to the floor, dragging her with him. Keeping low, he crawled to the wounded man, grabbed his collar and dragged him into the room, kicking the door shut as soon as Carlos was inside.

"Thank you," the man gasped, still clutching his bleeding leg as bullets popped through the door above them.

"You were blocking the door," Angel said, as he rolled Carlos away from the door and behind the safety of the brick walls of the room.

Still on autopilot, he tried to push the man's hand away from his wound, but Carlos whimpered and refused.

"Let me," Fiona said, kneeling beside him.

Angel realized he'd almost forgotten about her, she was so quiet. Sure, there had been her initial scream when the shooting began, but now she was controlled. Calm.

He glanced at her and reassessed his opinion. Not calm. Her pupils were dilated. The pulse in her neck jumped beneath her skin. Her hands shook. Freaking out was closer to the truth. But that was on the inside.

On the outside, she moved with gentle assurance, pushing Carlos's hand aside. Blood oozed but didn't spurt. The man would live.

She wasn't wiping out the bad guys, but she was solid. Controlled. Hell, he'd seen soldiers freak out under less pressure, and here she was, locked down in a gunfight and tending to the wounded as if there were no danger just on the other side of the wall.

"You got this?" he asked, making sure his assessment was correct.

"We're good. Go," Fiona said, her focus still on Carlos.

Angel rose. He had bigger issues—like how to escape without getting them killed.

"I think you'll live," Fiona said, smiling at the scared man on the floor.

"I am not so sure," Carlos replied through clenched teeth.

The sound of shouting penetrated the wooden door. Instinctively, Fiona ducked as the gunfire resumed. A few seconds later, the shooting stopped, and an ominous silence took its place.

"That doesn't bode well," Fiona said.

"No. It doesn't," Angel said. His tone chilled her. She glanced up from attending Carlos and her skin prickled with goose bumps. His face was expressionless. Not dark or broody. Not angry or grim. Certainly not scared.

And his eyes. She shuddered. It was like peering into a shark's pure black, soulless gaze.

She swallowed her fear, reminding herself that Angel was saving her butt and thankful he was on her side. "What next?" They were trapped. The only exits out of the studio were through the front and back doors. Worse, there were innocent bystanders in the crossfire.

Angel took a deep breath and turned his dark gaze to Carlos. "Where does that door lead?" he pointed to the other door with his thumb.

"Into a storage room."

"Is there any way out of there?"

"Another door that leads into the studio."

Fiona's goose bumps broke out with goose bumps. "The studio where all the men with guns are?"

"Yes."

That didn't sound healthy. "What'll we do?" she asked.

Angel pulled the gun from his belt. "There is no *we*. I'll take care of this."

Keeping low, he opened the door to the storage room, glanced in, and then entered. "Keep down. I'll be back in five," he said and shut the door behind him.

Fiona lay next to Carlos and waited. In less than a minute, gunfire erupted in the outer room, making her jump.

A vision of Tony raced across her mind. His chest soaked in blood. The way his eyes remained open, sightless.

Then it wasn't Tony. It was Angel. His chest penetrated by bullets. The life fading from him. She squeezed her eyes shut. "No," she whispered. "Don't die, Angel." She sent the plea skyward.

More gunfire and the almost simultaneous sound of cracking wood then the sound of a bullet as it hit the far wall.

Please be okay.

The shooting stopped and silence reigned. After a few seconds, Fiona rolled over onto her back, taking a moment to listen before sitting up. There was murmuring on the other side, but she couldn't make out who.

The door opened, and Angel walked through, his hair sticking up and his eyes dark.

But he was unharmed. Alive. That was all that mattered. Though weak with relief, Fiona jumped to her feet and surprised herself by wrapping her arms around the mercenary's neck. "Don't ever do anything that reckless again," she whispered, tasting the salt of his sweat on her lips. "I thought you were dead."

He hesitated, then pulled her close and squeezed her until she was breathless. His heart beat against her chest. "It wasn't reckless," he said, his voice low and husky. "I'm a professional."

She breathed deep, taking in the distinct smell of sweat and gunpowder. "Just…" She hesitated, searching for the words to describe the unexpected emotions that coursed through her.

There were no words. Nothing in the written language to describe the combination of fear, panic, admiration and relief that washed over her in waves. "Just don't," she finished.

Angel pulled back, his large hand cupping her cheek. His eyes met hers, but they were no longer unemotional. They were deeper. Richer. If she weren't careful, she'd get lost in those eyes.

"I'll try," he conceded.

Trying wasn't enough for Fiona. She wanted more. Wanted him to promise her. But she knew he wouldn't. He wasn't that kind of guy.

And that was why she needed him. "It'll have to do," she said, hating the concession.

Angel took a step back, and her arms slid to her side. She crossed them over her chest, hugging his heat close.

"What happened?" Carlos asked.

"I lived. They died," Angel said.

He said it like most people talked about the weather.

"And my people?"

"A few wounded, but okay," Angel said. "You might want to clear out, though, and not just from the station but from Bogotá. Montoya will come looking for us, and he'll do whatever it takes to get information on where we're going. Get your people and their families someplace safe."

The journalist flushed. "Help me up," he said, holding out his hand. Angel grabbed it, drawing him to his feet, and then helped him to a chair. "What about my station?" he asked Fiona. "I don't have time to get everything out. When Montoya comes here, and he will, he'll destroy the equipment or confiscate it. I'll lose everything."

Fiona bit her lip. Guilt gnawed at her but there wasn't anything she could do but live with it. The damage was done. "I'm sorry," she said. "When this is over, I'll do whatever I can to help replace the gear."

"And the footage?" Carlos asked.

Fiona scrubbed her face with her hands, frustrated at the turn of events. It seemed so simple when she went to Angel. Get the footage out. Everyone stayed safe. How hard could it be?

When did she become so naive?

She sighed into her palms then crossed her arms back over her chest. "Don't worry about that. Just get your people to safety," she said. "I know what he's capable of. I watched him gun down two people."

Angel touched her arm. "We need to leave," he said. He turned his gaze to Carlos. "Got a car?"

"No," he said. Looking at his still-oozing leg, his mouth turned up in a wry smile. "But I have a motorcycle. It's not like I'll be able to ride it—not with this leg, and besides, I owe you."

"You owe us? We led Montoya here," Fiona said.

Angel glared at her, but she ignored him. Besides, it wasn't as if she could take her words back.

"Let's say that I would like to see Montoya brought down," Carlos said. "Colombia needs change, both social and governmental. Montoya only makes change more difficult by using guns and intimidation to enforce the current structure.

"I do not want my children to grow up in a world of fear and chaos. Montoya must be stopped."

Angel recognized the words. "You support RADEC?"

Carlos hesitated then smiled. "The bike is inside the door. Get the tape out of here. Stop Montoya," he said, not answering Angel's question directly but still saying all he needed to say.

Fiona returned the smile then leaned down and kissed his cheek. "Thank you."

Angel took her hand. "Time to go."

She nodded. "How will you get away?" she asked Carlos.

"We're family here," the journalist replied. "And I have friends."

RADEC? Fiona wondered.

He continued, "We take care of each other." Reaching into his pocket, he tossed Angel the keys. Angel caught them in midair, and they headed toward the door.

"Fiona," Carlos said.

She hesitated.

"Can you stop Montoya?" Carlos asked. "Can you put him behind bars?"

"Yes," she said with a conviction she didn't feel.

To Angel, he said, "Take care of her. Make sure she keeps her promises."

"Of course," he said. Taking the lead, Angel crouched down, slipped into the studio, glanced around and then motioned for Fiona to follow. She hurried after him, half expecting to be shot on sight.

Most of the workers were still present but seemed too stunned to stop them. Behind them, Carlos shouted for help.

The bike was just where Carlos said. Red and chrome, it was built for speed. What her brother would call a crotch rocket.

Straddling the seat, Angel rolled it backward. "Can you follow directions?" he asked, once the bike was parallel with the still-closed door.

"Of course," Fiona replied.

"I am going to crank this up. You are going to open the door and hop on behind me. Fast. Then we're going to speed out of here. People might shoot at us. Do not fall off. Do not scream. Keep yourself pressed as close to me as possible. Can you do that?"

"Yes," Fiona said. Heart pounding, she put her hand on the door handle, ready to fling it open then move into position.

"And Fiona?" Angel said. His hand was on the key and his dark gaze bored into her, making her itch.

"Yes?"

"Keep low. Don't get shot."

She nodded. "I'll do my best."

He turned the ignition, and she flung open the door then jumped on behind him in one smooth motion. The bike sank with their combined weight, and Fiona wrapped her arms around Angel's waist, pressing herself against his back.

This is the worst idea ever, a voice in the back of her head whispered. She was a freaking shield.

She ignored the voice. There was no time for second guesses or doubt or making another choice. There was only the trust that Angel would get her out of this mess with her skin intact.

He'd done it so far.

He gunned the bike, and she clutched at him as they roared through the open doorway. To their left were three men. Before she had time to react, Angel spun the bike, using one leg to keep them from toppling over, and sped away in the opposite direction down the alley.

Behind them, the men yelled and gunfire sounded over their shouts. Fiona flinched, expecting to feel a bullet in the back with each passing heartbeat, but Angel yanked the bike from side to side, zigzagging to make them a harder target.

Fiona glued herself to Angel until there wasn't even air between them and prayed their luck would last.

She peeked over his shoulder as he sped up. The end of the alley loomed closer and, beyond that, a road with cars. A squeak of fear made its way past her lips before she could bury her face in Angel's back and cut the sound off.

"Hang on!" he shouted.

As if she needed to be told. She locked her hands together as the bike became airborne, cleared the curb and then hit the road with a thud. Around them, tires screeched, horns blared and there was the distinct sound of metal crunching.

But they were unharmed. "You okay?" Angel asked over his shoulder as he wove through the snarled traffic.

Fiona took a deep breath. Her heart beat a like a rabbit's, but otherwise she seemed intact. "I'm good."

Angel gave a quick nod then went up a gear, ignoring the shouts of angry drivers, the shriek of sirens and the speed limit as he headed away from the chaos they'd created.

Chapter 6

Angel slowed the bike, and Fiona peeked through her lashes into the setting sun directly ahead of them, and then at their surroundings.

They were in the middle of nowhere. No buildings. No houses. No local hotel. Just mile upon mile of dusty dirt road surrounded by the beginnings of jungle.

Desolation at its peak.

But on the upside, no cars and no people.

Angel's muscles flexed beneath her hands, and her mouth went dry as her fingertips skimmed the surface of his skin. Slowing, Angel turned the bike off the road.

She might be safe from Montoya, she realized, but safe from herself might be another matter.

She wasn't sure why Angel's proximity bothered her. He was fit. Handsome. Strong. But she'd dated a lot of men who fit that description, and none of them left her flushed and wanting.

But then none of them had risked their lives for her.

Altruism was a powerful aphrodisiac. Couple that with touching him all day—

Swallowing hard, she leaned back, putting what distance she could between them as he drove into the jungle until the road disappeared behind them.

"We'll camp here for the night."

Angel turned off the bike and dismounted. Fiona moved to follow and stopped with a whimper.

"You okay?" Angel asked, stretching.

"I think so," she said, lustful thoughts disappearing with the realization that her ass was numb and her legs were putty thanks to a day on the road, stopping only to fill the gas tank or purchase water and food.

"Here." He held out a hand. She eyed it then accepted the help, knowing there was no way she'd get off the bike otherwise. Stumbling, she fell into him.

Damn. He felt good beneath her palms and seemed annoyingly spry for spending the day in the driver's seat. He flashed her a bright white grin, and she rolled her eyes. How he managed to be mostly unspattered by bugs was beyond her comprehension.

"Careful, *grace*," Angel teased, as she regained her footing.

Surprised, she stopped midstep. "Did you just make a joke?" She'd barely seen him smile, must less say something that some might consider amusing.

He shrugged. "Call it what you want. Let's make a bed."

She raised a brow. "Nice variation, but you already tried that one. When we first met."

"Keeps me entertained," he said. Pulling a knife from his pocket, he went to the edge of the small clearing and began cutting fronds from a large bush.

Stretching to work out the kinks in her body, Fiona turned in a slow circle as Angel worked. The trees were thick, and the little clearing grew darker as the sun set behind the mountains.

A branch shifted, as if from the weight of some creature, and Fiona shivered. She hated the dark. Hated not being able to see what might be *out there,* waiting for her to drop her guard. As a child, she'd insisted on a night-light but had managed to break the habit as an adult. Still, to be out in the jungle at night brought back her childhood insecurities with a vengeance. "Any chance of a fire?" she asked, rubbing her arms as if cold when she was anything but chilled.

"No," Angel replied.

It figured. "I thought we were safe."

"We are, but it's hot as hell out, the humidity is almost one hundred percent, and we won't last long if we advertise our location." Angel gestured toward the pile of fronds next to him. "Start laying these down over there," he said, "lighter side up."

Fiona nodded, and in a few minutes had constructed a crude pallet.

Angel stood next to her. "Nice job."

"I guess." She thought it looked both hard and prickly.

"You never camped?"

"Sure, but my family's outings tended to involve a tent, fire, S'mores and, when we were older, cheap beer."

He grinned. "Think of this as hard-core camping."

"More like a survival course," she said.

Angel added a few more fronds to the bed. "Next time, I'll see what I can do to provide room service and thousand-count sheets."

Though she doubted he saw her eyes in the deepening dark, she glared at him. He loved this—the girly-girl reporter stuck in the middle of the jungle without her amenities.

Angel lay down on their makeshift bed. "Want to give her a try?" he asked, patting the space next to him. The sky was dark now, but she was sure that if she could see him better, he'd be wiggling his eyebrows in mock suggestion.

"I wouldn't miss it." She stuck her tongue out at him then lay down on the leaves. They were surprisingly comfortable, but there was no way she'd sleep tonight, not between the adrenaline, the fear, the humid night air, and a too-sexy mercenary lying next to her.

She almost groaned. Not even sore muscles could keep her from lusting after Angel.

Now is not the time, she reminded herself. Acting on lust would complicate things. He lived in Colombia. She lived in L.A. She dated intellectuals who liked the theatre. She was fairly sure that while he was smart, he'd never seen a musical.

Plus, there was his *"why am I helping you I must be crazy"* attitude and her desire to smack him every time he gave her a bad time.

So, lust was a bad idea. Even if the object of her affection was a hot, toned-beyond-belief mercenary who had saved her ass. Twice.

She needed to stay distant. Detached. Remember that she was a reporter and use that skill set to keep above her emotions.

"Tell me, how did you get a name like Angel? It's not common."

He shrugged. "It's just a name."

Damn, he was difficult to talk to sometimes. "What about your family?" she pressed.

"What about them?"

"I told you a little about mine. Camping. Cheap beer. What about yours? What did you do for vacation? Camp? Swim at the beach? What?"

For a few beats, there was nothing but silence. "I have two sisters, both younger. Married. Kids. Good stable lives." He spoke with what Fiona thought might be wistfulness if she were talking to anyone else.

"What about your parents?" she asked. "You do have them, don't you?"

"My dad cut out when Elena was born but my mom's still around. She lives in Arizona."

"Arizona? I thought you were from Colombia."

"My dad was. We moved back to the U.S. after he left," Angel said.

"Why did you come back?"

"Work."

More silence.

Fiona swallowed hard. Sharing time was over, there was no doubt about that. She wished it wasn't. She knew so little about the man next to her. Granted, Tony had trusted him and now she did, as well, but still there was so much unknown.

Where was his mother now? Alive? Dead? And girlfriends? Had he ever had one?

She suspected she might never know.

With a small sigh, she turned her back to Angel. The fronds shifted as he turned toward her, but that was where he stopped. No snuggling. No spooning. Still, he was so close that the heat from his skin warmed her. Her blood thrummed with desire, and a little voice in her head whispered that if she moved a few inches, she'd be in his arms.

Who would know?

She would, damn it.

Angel's breathing evened out as sleep claimed him, settling the dilemma.

Fiona turned over onto her stomach. Then onto her back. She counted stars. But sleep was elusive. She turned over again, this time, facing her rescuer.

She knew she'd never sleep with Angel next to her, and her nerves pulled so tight they threatened to snap like piano wire. With a sigh of resignation, she turned back to face the jungle and watch the eyes in the dark as they watched her.

* * *

The jungle came to life around them in the predawn. Staring into the dark with Fiona tucked into his side, Angel enjoyed the moment of unexpected contentment that came from being alone with her.

Directly above them, a bird called to its mate, and Angel raised a brow at the high-pitched screech. Fiona stirred next to him but didn't wake. Angel grinned. Her ability to sleep through the racket was both a rare gift and a potential problem.

His problem, though.

And he didn't want it to become hers. That's why she had him—to take care of the more lethal situations so she could sleep as soundly as a child. Granted, this would all be easier if she was more savvy, but he realized he liked her occasional bouts of naivety. It was refreshing.

More animals woke around them and the noise level steadily increased. He knew he should wake Fiona, but instead he pulled her closer. She snuggled into the crook of his arm. Let her sleep, he told himself. He'd have to wake her up soon enough, and then the running would start all over again.

How was he going to avoid Montoya? Keep Fiona safe and get the tape to where it would do the most good?

Now that the day ahead was in his thoughts, worries preoccupied his mind. Escaping Montoya's grasp was going to be tough because it wasn't just Montoya and his goons they had to avoid. It was the entire population of Colombia. Kidnappings were a daily occurrence, and the fact that they had a motorcycle made them targets. People wanted more money, a better life, and they were willing to take what they wanted with little thought to who they hurt.

He ran scenarios through his head but none gave him the ending he wanted.

Carefully, Angel brushed his lips across Fiona's hair. Despite the abuse of coloring, it was soft against his mouth.

Would exposing Montoya make that much of a difference to the country? he wondered. Was it worth putting Fiona in danger?

He sighed. Did it matter? There was no choice anymore.

They were on the run, and until he got her out of the country, neither was safe. He hoped she was up to the challenge. She was tough. There was no doubting that. She'd been through hell and still carried on. But would that strength last?

The bird screeched again, and this time Fiona stirred and blinked, adjusting to her situation and location.

"Morning," Angel said. Her face was creased from both the leaves and sleeping against his shirt, her hair was snarled, and she had sleep in her eyes.

She was still sexy as hell.

"Morning," Fiona said, her mouth just inches from his. She smiled at him, a slow sleepy grin that begged for a kiss. "Any chance we could get room service to bring coffee?"

"I'll see what I can do," Angel whispered, mesmerized by her mouth. "But we might have to tip in bananas."

She sighed, snuggled closer then stopped as if just realizing what she was doing. She held her breath, staring at him, her eyes wide and wanting.

Damn, he wanted to kiss her, and he knew—his gut knew—she wanted his kiss. He touched her hair, stroked the black strands. "Fiona," he whispered her name.

And it struck him. Last night was the first night since Isabel died that he hadn't thought of his fiancée. Today was the first morning he'd woken up with someone else in his arms.

And he wasn't sure how he felt about that. Sad. Relieved.

Guilty as hell.

He rolled away, and the smooth sides of Isabel's ring dug into his skin with a surprising sharpness.

"What is it?" Fiona asked, one arm under her head as she watched him, confused. "What's wrong?"

Angel shook his head. God help him, he needed Fiona. Needed to feel her naked skin against his. Needed to make love to her.

Needed to feel something he hadn't felt in over two years.

But not like this. Not with his emotions running amuck and out of control. Not with memories of Isabel still over him like a shadow.

Angel sat up.

"Nothing's wrong," he said. At least not with you. "We should get moving. We have a long day ahead of us."

Her brows knit in confusion, and her eyes flashed disappointment. Both reactions were gone as quickly as they'd appeared. She rolled away and onto her knees. "Okay, where are we going?"

He had to give her credit. She didn't pout or complain. Just got down to business. At least one of them had their head squared away, though it should have been him. "I thought about that last night, and we're heading to the coast."

He cleared away a spot on the ground, exposing the rich dirt beneath. "We're taking back roads, but in case something happens to me—"

Fiona stiffened, but Angel continued, "If something happens, you need to know where to go."

Using a stick, he drew a rough map of Colombia. "This is us." He made a crosshatch mark in the dirt. "This is the main road to the Pacific coast and the city of Buenaventura. When you get there, go to Marina Blanco de la Roca. It's at the south end of the city."

"What's there?" Fiona asked.

"My sailboat. The *Last Ditch Effort.*"

Fiona raised a brow. "Comforting name."

"I was going for descriptive," he replied. "Go at night and you shouldn't run into anyone. If you run into the marina people, tell them you're meeting me there. The combination on the lock to the cabin is seven-one-three."

The date he met Isabel.

Fiona nodded but didn't seem as sure as he hoped. "You can do this," he assured her.

"I know," she said. "Let's just not let it come to that. Agreed?"

Now it was Angel who nodded. "Agreed."

A few minutes later, they were on the road, driving slowly to avoid potholes. Thirty minutes later, they were in the foothills of the Andes. Cresting another small hill, Angel glanced into the valley below. Beneath them was a small town. He glanced at the gas gauge, hovering over E, and hoped the locals were friendly. "We're going in," Angel said. "I don't want you to speak any English if anyone is within earshot."

"Not a problem," Fiona replied.

They puttered into the town. The cement and adobe buildings were old. Crumbling. The outsides were tagged with what Angel knew were various gang symbols.

Not good.

Though it was early, people were already walking the street, going to work, shopping, whatever it took to get them through the day. And getting through the day seemed to be the attitude. Most towns were happy to see visitors. These people ignored them or, in a few cases, glared at them.

Great.

He also realized they were riding the only motorized vehicle in sight. Dammit, could it get much more complicated?

"Is this safe?" Fiona whispered. "They don't look too friendly."

"I know," Angel said. "But we don't have a choice. We need gas."

"If there's any here."

He didn't miss the hint of fear in her voice. "Don't worry," he said, slowing as they came to an intersection in the dirt road. "Let me do the talking. We'll get in and get out. No problem."

"Okay," she said.

Time to get this over with, Angel told himself. Stopping, he nodded toward a man that walked past. *"Buenos dias, señor. Como esta—"*

The man glanced at him, didn't utter a word and kept going.

"That went well," Fiona muttered under her breath.

"Buenos dias, señora," Angel said as a woman passed them. He held out a coin worth five pesos.

She stopped. *"¿Qué?"*

What? That was to the point. *"¿Gasolina?"*

She snatched the coin and pointed down the street. *"El mercado. Prequnte por Abram."*

"Gracias."

"De nada." And she went on her way, stuffing the coin in her pocket.

"No gas station but they have Abram," Fiona whispered, incredulous. "Do you think she was telling the truth?"

"I hope so," Angel replied. Of course, if Montoya's intel reached here first, she might be on her way to the police.

Even if she wasn't, there was still the local gang to worry about. It was a sure bet they were aware of him and Fiona, and it wouldn't take long before they'd come around, hoping to use him and Fiona as their way to easy money.

Angel hoped to be long gone by then.

Fiona sighed and wrapped her arms around him, resting her head against his back.

It felt good.

Which was *not* good, Angel told himself. Desire was a distraction. Keeping the bike in low gear, he headed toward the market the woman mentioned. Two streets down, he saw the sign and pulled in front. The outside of the market was a mishmash of assorted used plywood and rusted tin. Turning off the motorcycle, he pocketed the keys.

"Do I wait here or come with you?" Fiona whispered.

"Stand over here. Look inconspicuous and watch the bike," he replied. "If anyone approaches either you or the bike, yell. I don't care if it's a five-year-old kid with his hand out. You yell." He hated leaving her by herself, but leaving the bike alone was like saying, "Steal me," and they needed the vehicle.

Luckily, the market was small and he'd be within earshot no matter where he went.

Fiona dismounted, planted her back against the wall, hands in her pockets, and looked anything but relaxed.

Angel headed into the market. It wasn't much. A few booths with produce. One with chicken. All tended by women. In the middle was a booth crammed with everything from gum to wrenches to cigarettes. And in the midst of the clutter was a short, bone-thin man dressed in a dirty pair of Levi's jeans and a faded T-shirt that proclaimed him an Official Bikini Inspector.

Abram. He was sure of it.

"Buenos dias," Angel said. *"Necesito la gasolina."*

The man gave a slow nod and an even slower jack-o'-lantern smile. *"¿Cuánto?"*

"Seis litros."

The old man frowned. Angel guessed that six liters of gas was barely worth his time, but he also knew that no shopkeeper turned away money.

"Sesenta pesos," the shopkeeper said, grinning. Angel recognized the barter dance and fought the urge to roll his eyes. He didn't have time for this. Shrugging, he took sixty pesos from his pocket and pressed them into the old man's open palm.

The man's grin changed to a frown, but he pocketed the bills, obviously liking easy money more than the thrill of negotiation. He motioned for Angel to follow.

They went around the back of the ramshackle booth and Angel

glanced back toward Fiona. He couldn't see her. He turned to the man, wanting to get back to Fiona as soon as possible. The gas was in a white five-gallon bucket that, according to its label, once held mayonnaise.

He hoped Abram cleaned the bucket prior to filling it.

"Esto bien," Abram said, anticipating the question.

Angel hefted it up. The bucket was maybe a quarter full. There were perhaps three liters. Nowhere close to six.

Abram grinned. *"¿Es justo, no?"*

Is it fair? He had to be kidding. *"Es bueno,"* Angel said through gritted teeth, promising that if he ever returned to this hellhole people called home, he'd take a few minutes to wipe the smug smile off of Abram's face.

But the vendor knew he was in a hurry and that meant there wasn't time for anything but getting the gas and leaving. Angel put the lid on the container and that's when he heard Fiona.

"Angel!"

"Dammit!" Dropping the bucket, Angel drew his gun from beneath his shirt. He bolted toward the front of the market. In the doorway, silhouetted by the morning sun, was the scene Angel had dreaded might happen.

Fiona was on the ground. Three men, all wearing black pants and matching black shirts with red bandanas wrapped around their left biceps, stood around her. A fourth straddled her, pulling at her clothes as she clawed and punched, trying to get away.

Pure, cold rage consumed Angel, and he moved with no thought but to kill them all.

He was almost on them when they looked up, eyes wide and grins wider. They froze for a heartbeat then went for their guns. Their hesitation was all Angel needed. He raised his weapon and fired first. The bullet slammed into the shoulder of the closest man, knocking him off his feet.

Angel barely broke stride as he grabbed another by the wrist, locked the man's elbow against his forearm, and pulled his arm up and backward, pushing him to his knees at the same time. The man was halfway to the ground when his shoulder dislocated with a distinct popping sound. Angel held firm until he felt the distinctive *snap* as the bone and the joint fractured. He let go and the man dropped, screaming.

Cool rage driving him, Angel pivoted. The third assailant was in the middle of raising his weapon. Angel grabbed his wrist and twisted hard. It snapped in less than a second, and the gun fell away while the man joined his friend on the ground.

Now for the fourth.

It took every ounce of control to not simply grab the man by the head and break his neck, but Fiona had seen enough, been through enough, and he didn't want her to see him as a murderer.

He was the hero, dammit. Grabbing the man by the collar, he yanked him off Fiona, tossed him to the ground, and then kicked him in the ribs.

"Angel, look out!" Fiona screamed, looking past him.

Even as she screamed, the fifth, unseen man was already on him, knife drawn. Angel hit the ground hard, grabbing the man's knife hand on the way down and twisting his wrist until the blade clattered to the ground

They grappled, each seeking the advantage. Angel dripped with sweat; if he failed, Fiona would be at the mercy of the gang, and *mercy* would not be their operative word.

Suddenly, the man collapsed on top of him. Angel pushed him off. Fiona stood above him with a brick in her hand.

Eyes narrowed and a scowl on her mouth, she looked pissed, but with the exception of a few scratches, appeared unharmed.

"Thanks," he said, rising.

"My pleasure." She dropped the brick on the chest of the unconscious bandit and kicked him in the kidney. "Gas?" she asked.

The shopkeeper ran forward with the purchased gas, his expression fearful. Angel wasn't sure if it was fear of him or the bandits, and he didn't care. He started filling the tank.

A car's backfire made him jump.

Fiona tugged on his arm. "We have company."

Angel saw an ancient Volkswagen coming down the street. Two men hung from the rear windows, guns waving as they bore down on the bike.

"Dammit." Dropping the gas, Angel twisted the cap back on the tank and jumped on. Fiona scooted on behind, wrapping her arms around him. "Hang on!" Angel shouted and gunned the engine. The bike kicked up dust as they took off down the road with the car in pursuit.

Chapter 7

Fiona glanced past Angel's shoulder and into the rearview mirror. Despite the amazing amount of rust on the body of the small car, the overload of bodies taking up the interior, and the black smoke trailing from the exhaust, the gang members still trailed them. The men hooted and yelled, their shouts growing closer even as Angel pushed the motorcycle to its highest speed. She didn't know what was under the rusty hood but it sure as hell wasn't a Volkswagen engine.

She didn't doubt that this ploy worked with unfortunate tourists—drive a car with a crappy exterior and people thought they had the upper hand. By the time they realized they'd been fooled, they were sitting in a hut somewhere waiting for their relatives to pay a heavy ransom.

"Angel!" Fiona coughed and gagged as a bug flew down her throat. "They're gaining."

"I know," he yelled, the wind whipping his voice away even as it reached her ears.

Of course, he does, she thought. He's Angel. He knows everything, and until now it seemed there wasn't a situation he couldn't survive. But a car full of gangsters that knew the locale, coupled with a motorcycle that wouldn't last much longer, worked against him on all levels.

A bang sounded and Fiona instinctively ducked her head. A projectile screamed past them. Fiona's heart broke into a sprint, fear rolled over her and she forgot to breathe. That was close. Too damned close and this time, there wasn't a brick wall to provide cover.

Immediately, Angel turned the bike, sending it into a zigzag pattern much as he had in the alley yesterday. A second shot sounded, kicking up the dirt in front of them. Fiona tightened her grip around Angel's waist and sent a prayer to anyone who might be listening to keep them safe.

"I need a head count," Angel shouted. "Can you do that?"

"Yes," Fiona shouted back. Steeling herself, she looked over her shoulder. One man hung out the back window, a gun in his grip. Two more were in the seat next to him. Three sat up front. All wore black shirts and sported the red bandanas.

The man in the passenger seat unrolled his window to aim a rifle at them. She turned away as he fired. Just once, she'd like to meet someone in Colombia—besides Angel—who didn't want to see her dead.

"We have six," Fiona shouted. "Three in front and three in the back."

"Too many to fight," Angel shouted over his shoulder. "You're going to have to shoot the car."

"What?" He wanted her to shoot a car? Who did he think she was, James Bond?

"Just do it!"

The odds she'd hit anything seemed unlikely, but there wasn't much choice. One hand clutching Angel, she reached down and pulled the gun from the side pocket of her cargo pants. It wasn't a large weapon, but trying to balance the weight and fire seemed ten times more difficult on a moving bike.

Twenty times harder if she let herself think about the fact that the gangsters were going to fire back.

"Squeeze the trigger. Don't pull it," Angel said, his head tilted so his mouth was closer to her ear. "And give me a heads-up so I'll know it's coming."

"Got it." Shoving all doubt to the back of her head, she turned enough to put the car full of men in her sights. "Don't freak," she murmured to herself. "Don't scream. And don't drop the gun."

Aiming for the front of the car, and what she hoped was the radiator, she yelled, "One. Two. Three!" Holding her breath, she squeezed the trigger. Her arm flew upward with the kickback and the bike wobbled then straightened. She clutched the gun, forcing her fingers to retain their grip even as fire shot down her arm.

"You all right?" Angel asked.

Gingerly, Fiona lowered her arm. She'd be sore later. "I'm fine."

"Did you get them?"

Gunfire answered before she could reply and Fiona ducked. A bullet whizzed past her ear. "Crap!"

Worse, the car didn't seem any farther away. She hadn't done a thing except piss them off.

They were angry? She frowned. They weren't the ones running for their lives. They didn't know anger. Hand shaking with pain, she raised the gun again. "Hang on", she yelled. "Firing!"

The gun kicked, but this time she was ready and she worked to absorb the brunt of the kickback.

Still, the car full of gangsters kept coming. Dammit, she cursed herself. She couldn't hit anything. At least, not anything important.

She was a journalist. Not a soldier. She should be driving the motorcycle, not trying to kill the bad guy. She took a deep breath and steeled her jaw. Reporter or not, she needed to channel her inner überbitch and stop the bad guys. She raised the gun. Keeping her eye on her chosen target, the windshield, she refused to even blink. "Firing."

The windshield shattered with a spray of red, and the Volkswagen careened across the road and into the bushes. "I did it!" she screamed, though she wasn't sure if she was excited at the fact that she hit something or if she wanted to throw up since the something she'd hit was a person. Her stomach clenched tight, and she suspected the latter option might win out.

Angel slowed the bike, glancing at the carnage in his rearview mirror. "Nice job," he said and sped back up.

Fiona swallowed hard, willing her stomach to relax. He was a gangster, she reminded herself. He would have killed you. Killed Angel. You did what had to be done.

Gun still in her hand, she wrapped her arm back around Angel and rested her head against his back, not caring if it bothered him. Instead, he slipped the gun from her fingers and into his pocket.

Behind her closed eyes, she saw the window shatter again. The blood. "Angel, pull over." She put her hand over her mouth.

He kept going.

"Now!"

He pulled over to the side of the road, and as soon as the bike stopped, Fiona slid off the back, fell to her knees, and lost what little food was in her stomach.

When the heaving was finished, she realized that Angel was holding her hair back. She sat up, sweaty and out of breath. "I'm done."

He let go of her hair and produced a small water bottle from one of his pockets. "It's warm," he said, handing it to her.

"Don't care." Grateful, she rinsed her mouth and spat the water out. "I'm sorry. I've never shot someone before."

"I know." Angel knelt beside her. "You did good. Thank you."

She tried to smile. "Really? I was just trying to even us up in the 'who saves who' department."

Angel smiled back. "You can joke, but I wasn't sure you could do it. It was a tough decision, but you did what was needed to keep us both safe."

Fiona warmed at the praise, trying not to appear too pleased.

Angel stroked her cheek with his thumb. "Are you going to be sick again?"

She hesitated as she listened to her body. Her stomach was empty, and though she wouldn't describe her emotional state as calm, she was done being sick. "I'll be fine."

"Good," he said, kindness replaced with the all-business attitude she knew so well. "We need to get moving." He took her elbow and helped her to her feet.

As if on cue, the sound of an approaching car caught their attention. Fiona saw the Volkswagen crest the hill. "You have got to be kidding me."

Angel ran for the bike. "Go!" She jumped on, and the bike fishtailed as they went from zero to full speed in ten seconds. Once again, she glanced over her shoulder. The bike might have been built for speed, but they'd lost distance when they stopped, and it didn't look like they were going to keep ahead. Not this time. In seconds, the car full of gangsters was within a few feet. Men hung out the windows. No weapons this time, though.

Instead, they reached for her. The one in the back leaned farther. His fingers brushed her shirt. Then her hair, managing to grip a few strands. Fiona jerked her head, eyes watering as he tore the strands free. "Angel!"

"Hang on," he shouted and pulled off the road and into the trees. She turned her head, not wanting to watch when Angel plowed them into a tree. Behind them, the Volkswagen screeched to a halt, and a barrage of gunshots exploded around them, sending bark from nearby trees flying into them.

Angel turned the bike uphill, the engine whining with strain and slowing despite his efforts to maintain speed as they went around brush and trees.

A final gunshot echoed through the trees and Fiona turned. Despite the gunshot, the gangsters were no longer visible. She breathed a sigh of relief and turned just in time to see the ground drop away in front of them and to feel the bike go airborne.

I've killed us both. It was Angel's first thought when the front wheel of the motorcycle left the ground. The regret that consumed him was instant.

But there was no time to think or feel. There was only time to act and assess the situation. Luckily, it was less of a cliff and more of a steep hill. He leaned back, trying to keep their combined weight off the front fork so they wouldn't somersault when the tire hit the ground.

The front tire connected with a thud that made Angel's jaw snap shut and his head snap forward. The back tire continued to lift.

He leaned back farther, pushing Fiona with him.

The bike stabilized beneath them, and Angel worked to keep it under control. But there was no stopping the vehicle. Not without laying it down. The hill was too steep and the rocks too loose, and even staying upright was precarious and almost impossible.

"Angel!" Fiona screamed in his ear.

He turned his attention in front of them at the panic in her voice and saw nothing but air. "Son of a bitch," he swore. He hadn't saved them from going over a cliff. He'd simply delayed it. And at the bottom was only who knew what. Probably big damned rocks.

There was no choice now. He'd have to lay the bike down to

keep them from going over. Fiona squeaked in his ear, and her grip tightened.

"Get ready to roll away," he shouted over his shoulder. "Go limp."

He didn't give her time to reply as he shifted to neutral, applied the brake, and leaned hard to the side. The bike slid out from under them. He steered into it then let go, letting momentum carry it away and down the hill. Then the world became a painful combination of dirt and rocks coupled with the occasional flash of blue sky as he rolled.

When he stopped moving, he realized he was only a few feet from the edge of the cliff. Taking a deep breath, he lay motionless and took stock of his body. Flexed his legs. Arms. Shifted his torso. Slowly, he moved his head from side to side. His vision remained stable. Bruises. Abrasions. He was sure he'd feel like hell tomorrow.

But nothing broken.

A groan caught his attention.

He rolled over toward the sound. Fiona was only a few feet away. She tried to sit up.

"Hold still," Angel said, crawling to her side. Quickly, he ran his hands over her, testing her extremities for breaks. She appeared intact and in roughly the same condition as himself. "Let me see your eyes," he said, kneeling next to her.

She blinked up at him, her blue eyes matching the sky above them.

"Was that necessary?" she asked.

"Dumping the bike?"

"What do you think?" she asked.

"I see your sense of sarcasm wasn't damaged," Angel said, noting that her pupils were the same size, which meant that it was doubtful she had a concussion. "But yes, it was necessary. Unless you had a burning urge to take a flying leap off a cliff."

"Point taken." Fiona tried to sit up and grimaced, her breath hissing through her teeth. Angel placed a hand under her back and helped her rise to a sitting position.

"Think they'll come after us?" she asked, rubbing her head and taking in their surroundings.

"Yes," he replied. There was no way their pursuers would let them leave without a fight. Kidnapping was a form of employment in Colombia, and when observed in that light, he and Fiona were a year's wages. He stood and offered Fiona his hand.

Her fingers wrapped around his, and he helped her to her feet. She stumbled into him, and he took a step backward, trying to keep them both balanced, and ended up with her in his arms.

The heat between them was instant and palpable and both froze. Slowly, Fiona put her hand against Angel's chest then raised her chin until her eyes met his.

Her eyes filled with something familiar. Desire.

Intense. Burning. Unexpected.

"Angel." She said his name like a lover. "I seem to keep falling into you."

He stood on the edge of a cliff with all of creation before him, and yet, he couldn't seem to find air enough to breathe. It's adrenaline, Angel told himself. Just adrenaline. The normal reaction to escaping death.

But it isn't just adrenaline. It's more. Or becoming more.

Confused, Angel forced himself to take a breath. No matter what his subconscious thought, he wasn't sure he wanted *more*. He'd loved before, and it had almost killed him when he lost it.

But this is Fiona, not Isabel, the voice whispered.

He took another breath. Fiona. Good-hearted. Tenacious. A huge pain in his ass.

More.

Angel tried to step away from Fiona, but if breathing was hard, leaving Fiona's heat was harder. Instead, the voice won out, and he found his hands sweeping up her sides and skimming her neck. Her skin was like silk. Velvet. He wanted to mark it with his mouth then kiss away the damage.

He cupped her face. Fiona stared at him. *Into* him.

Just like she always seemed to when he least expected it.

"Fiona." He whispered her name.

She responded by winding her fingers in his hair and pulling his mouth to hers, kissing him as if it were the last kiss she might ever know.

God help him, he was helpless to deny her. Helpless to deny himself any longer. Helpless to do anything but meet her passion with his own.

Groaning, he teased her mouth with his tongue, tracing her lower lip, and pulled her closer. Her hands slipped out of his hair and down to his chest, crumpling his wrinkled shirt in her grip as she demanded *more*.

And *more* was what he wanted to give her. Especially time. He could spend hours kissing her. Days exploring Fiona. He twisted her hair around his clenched fist and a sudden, unexpected noise caught his attention.

A snapping branch. Brush shaking. His desire died as suddenly as it had flared to life. "Shhh," he whispered, his mouth still touching hers.

He glanced past her and up the hill.

No dark silhouette appeared on the ledge above them, but his gut and experience told him that they had less than a minute to act.

"What is it?" Fiona whispered.

He gave her a quick kiss, wishing they had time. Toothbrushes. Baths. A change of clothes.

A bed.

But right now, they had to run. "They're almost here. Time to leave."

Her eyes grew wide as fear replaced desire. "Where to?" she asked, looking at him as if he had all the answers.

He gestured toward the cliff. "Let's get the hell out of here. Take this." He handed her one of the guns.

She grabbed it and stuck it in her pocket.

Being careful not to lose their footing on the loose rocks that littered the edge of the drop, they peered over the edge. The top half of the drop was a combination of rock and dirt with the occasional tree root jutting out. Below that was solid rock.

Of course, forty feet below that was a river filled with rocks— a precursor to white water, judging from the sound coming from around the bend downstream.

"Oh, hell," Fiona groaned.

He didn't disagree. Getting across would be a challenge, but it was the best course to deter their followers. That and leaving the motorcycle as a consolation prize. "Could be worse," Angel said.

"How?" Her tone was one of disbelief.

"Could be a longer climb and no soft water beneath," Angel said. He turned to her. "You can climb, can't you?"

"I've climbed the rock wall at the gym," Fiona answered, her attention still on the river below.

"Not quite the same."

She leaned a little farther over, and he thought her skin went a shade paler. "Oh, I figured that out."

"I'll go first," Angel said. "And help guide you."

"Goody."

He ignored the sarcasm and lowered himself over the edge, grabbing a tree root for balance as he searched for foot placement in the loose dirt.

Another foot and he'd have Fiona follow him.

Dirt rained on his head, and he looked up to see Fiona lowering herself toward him.

"Not yet," he called.

"They're here," Fiona called.

"Crap." There was no time to test for footholds, if there ever had been. Now it was a race to see if they could get to the safety of the river before their pursuers shot them from above. Angel hurried downward but Fiona was faster and lighter, and within seconds she was next to him.

Her skin was smudged with dirt and her cheek bruised. She looked as if she was screaming inside—he knew the feeling—but she moved as if she wasn't on the verge of turning into a ball of weeping mush.

Voices called out in Spanish. One argued to shoot them where they hung on the wall. Another wanted to force them to climb back up so they could be properly tortured.

He and Fiona had a few seconds to act, but little more. Familiar, chilly resolution washed over Angel and he let it consume him as he ticked over their few options in his head. Climb up. *Be tortured and shot.* Climb Down. *Be shot.*

Jump. *Possibly drown or hit a rock.*

"Fiona," he whispered. "Jump."

She peered down beneath her feet and her grip on the rock tightened. "I can't."

"No choice and no time to argue," he replied, keeping his voice low. "You'll go first. I know it's high, but you need to look down. Aim for a spot that looks deep. Push away. Hit that mark."

"I…" Her mouth opened and closed.

Her panic was close to the surface now, but he didn't give a damn. "Do it or I'll toss you off myself."

She took a deep breath.

Good girl.

Glancing down, she pushed away from the cliff and to the left. There was a splash and, seconds later, shouts from above.

Angel didn't have time to pick a point of entry. He jumped.

Keeping his legs pressed together and his body straight for minimal impact, he prayed for the best.

The sound of gunfire followed his fall then disappeared as the water swallowed him. Immediately, he spread his legs and arms outward to slow his descent then pushed his way toward the area where Fiona had entered the water.

He broke the surface and the gunfire resumed. Bullets peppered the water around him, and he ducked under, swimming hard away from the cliff.

When he surfaced again, Fiona was nowhere in sight.

Chapter 8

"Fiona!"

There was no response, just the sound of rushing water, shouts from the men and gunfire. Angel reached for his weapon. It was gone. He hoped to hell Fiona had hers.

"Damn it." Bullets peppered the water again. He took another deep breath and dove for the river bottom. Visibility was five feet in any direction but he took only a few seconds to search for his weapon. It was nowhere. Frustrated, he swam with the current, remaining beneath the water until his lungs burned.

He pushed upward again, treading water as the current swept him downriver. Spinning around, he was surprised to see that the gang members were considerably smaller. The river was faster than he thought. Which meant Fiona was farther away.

Still treading water, he slipped around a curve in the river, and the men disappeared from sight.

That was one problem solved. For now.

That left only Fiona.

"Where the hell are you," he muttered, scanning both the water around him and then the shoreline.

There was no sign of her.

"Fiona!" He called her name but the words were lost as he was carried downstream and the sound of white water intensified. Damn it, he had to find her before the water grew deadly. She was strong, and he had no doubt she would keep her wits about her, but something like this river required more than good intentions and a cool head.

It required brute strength. If he didn't find her soon—

Stop it.

He knew that hopeless situations were rarely that, but with each second, the sense that he might fail grew stronger.

Isabel.

The memory of her death flashed through his thoughts, but he refused to let it rock him. Now was not the time. Not when Fiona's life was on the line.

Still, there was no sign of her. It didn't matter. He'd find her simply because he wouldn't allow another option. He grabbed on to a large rock to stop his progress downstream. It was slick with moss and slime, but he hauled himself onto it to gain a better vantage. A flicker of movement downstream caught his eyes. But what? It was hard to tell, and he promised himself that when he had a chance, he'd buy Fiona something bright to wear. Something besides black.

Shading his view with a hand above his eyes, he caught a flash of pale flesh.

"Fiona!" He slid back into the frigid water and headed toward her, never taking his eyes off his target. She went under, and for a moment he was sure his heart had stopped.

She surfaced, arms flailing, and his heart resumed again. Then there was no longer any thought. No worry. Just Fiona and his burning need to get to her.

Thirty feet. "Hang on," he called out. "Feet first!"

She spun in the water, her expression as she briefly faced him one of determination as the river turned into white water around her.

He wasn't surprised at her inner strength. Once, he might have been. But no longer. She was tougher than he'd thought. Probably tougher than most people gave her credit for being.

He swam harder, determined to catch her. Everything she'd been through was terrifying. Life threatening. But they'd been dealing with men. He could predict the actions of men. Kill them. Sometimes bargain.

Twenty feet.

The river was Mother Nature. Nature wasn't forgiving. Wasn't kind. There was no reasoning. Just live or die.

And Fiona knew it. She clawed for something solid, reaching for the rocks, but the current was strong and her hands found no purchase on the slick surface. Instead, she crashed against the stone—

Angel flinched.

—she bounced off—

He flinched again.

—and she crashed into another rock only a few feet away. Her head thumped against the side, and then she slid under the water.

Ten feet.

This time, she didn't rise back to the surface.

Angel's pulse pounded in his ears and time seemed to slow as he dove under, searching. She floated a few feet ahead of him. He grabbed her shirt, pulling her limp body to the surface.

"Fiona." She remained unconscious. A dead weight. But breathing. Adrenaline pumped through his body, and he pulled her to him, her back against his chest. The river sped along. He couldn't fight the water, but he could use it.

Swimming perpendicular to the current, he scanned for a safe area as he headed for the bank.

Ahead was a small beach. The river held them, but Angel refused to let it win. He would beat nature. He'd done it before, and he'd do it now. It wasn't just his life but Fiona's, and he'd be dammed if he'd let her down now.

His muscles screamed and each breath burned in his chest, but he kept his eyes on the beach, willing his body to continue.

His feet hit the rocky bottom, and he stumbled in fatigue and relief. Carrying Fiona in his arms, he dragged himself to the river's edge and laid her on the shore. Gently, he pushed her hair away from her face. "Wake up." He patted her cheek.

She remained limp with the only sign of life her steady breathing. If she didn't wake up—

Not an option.

"Fiona." He whispered her name, calling to her, begging her with the single word to open her eyes because if she didn't, he wasn't sure what he would do.

She groaned, her eyelids flickered and she opened her eyes. "My head hurts."

She was alive and awake. Relief flooded Angel, and he collapsed beside her.

Fiona turned toward Angel, but the small movement only increased the throbbing in her head, making her gasp.

What the hell was going on? Disoriented and confused, she blinked at the sky that swirled above her. Her heart pounded, and she breathed deep and exhaled until the world returned to normal.

Being careful to keep her head as still as possible, Fiona rolled over. Angel's clothes were soaking wet and clung to him like a second skin. She realized she was wet, as well, and memory flooded back.

The chase. Jumping into the water and the sudden, intense

panic as the river sucked her in and closed over her head. Relief as it spit her upward just as fast.

Then there was swimming. Determination to reach the other side of the river without dashing herself against the rocks or getting a bullet in her head.

The gangsters.

She sat up. The world did a quick three-sixty, the sunlight dimmed and her head throbbed, but she took a deep breath and ignored it all. There were problems more pressing than pain.

"Where's my gun?" she muttered. Her pocket was empty.

Angel turned over with a sigh. "I lost mine, too." He turned back. "We'll get more. It's Colombia."

"Damn river," she said. They needed the weapons. They couldn't afford to lose things—

Horror rushed through her, and the throbbing in her head increased. "The tape. Where's the tape?"

Angel sat up.

Her hands scrambling and shaking, Fiona unzipped her pocket and reached inside. Her fingertips touched something hard. Plastic. Square. Relief flowed through her, and she pulled out the video.

"Do not scare me like that," Angel said, his jaw tight.

She nodded. "Sorry."

"Is it okay?"

"It's wet." That was never a good thing.

"Is it ruined?"

Fiona turned it over in her hand, but that told her nothing. "I'm not sure," she said. "It's not soaked all the way through." She shook the case next to her ear. "I don't hear water."

"It's the pants," Angel explained. "Military issue. Not waterproof, but they do provide some resistance to liquid."

That helped. "We shouldn't try to watch it. Not before the tape experts at my station have a chance to analyze it."

"Your station? When did we decide to go there?"

Fiona shrugged, not sure when she'd come to that conclusion, but it seemed logical. "We have to go somewhere, and I think it makes the most sense. I trust them, and they'll have a vested interest in making sure this story gets out." He didn't look convinced. "I'm open to suggestions if you have a better idea."

He pressed a finger to the bridge of his nose. "Where is this TV station?"

"Los Angeles."

"Figures," he said, looking as if the mere thought gave him a headache.

She almost asked if he had a problem with LA but clamped her mouth shut, deciding that she didn't care. Later, she might. But not now.

Fiona put the tape back in her pocket. Carefully she tried to rise and hissed in pain as the throbbing in her head transformed into the white-hot-knife metaphor she'd heard about but never experienced until now.

"Hold still." Angel kneeled in front of her and pushed her hair aside. His fingers grazed the knot on her head and the breath hissed through Fiona's teeth as the throbbing increased.

"Sorry," Angel said.

"S'okay."

She gritted her teeth as he examined her. "Well? Is it bad?"

"You tell me."

"It hurts like hell."

"Then it's bad." He turned her head until she faced directly into the sunlight, then he looked into her eyes. His intense stare made her squirm, but Fiona didn't entertain the idea it was romantic. He was checking for a concussion, but it was going to be difficult to tell in this light.

"How do you feel?" he asked. "Any nausea? Dizziness?"

"Didn't we just have this conversation?" Fiona asked. She

was beginning to feel like a heroine in a bad movie. The kind who required rescue every twenty minutes, leaving the audience to wonder why the hero wanted to save someone so ignorant and foolish.

"We did," Angel said. Rising, he offered her a hand. "Which is my worry. You've had more than one close call today."

Letting him help her, Fiona rose, taking care not to move too fast. The world tipped and swayed but held firm when she stopped midway, bent over with her hands on her knees.

"You're about to fall over." Angel said, his hand on her lower back. "Let me help you."

"I'm fine." Shaking him off, she slowly finished rising. "See," she said, forcing her voice to remain steady. "All better."

"Liar," Angel said.

She smiled. He pushed her hair away from her cheek and tucked it behind her ear. "We've got to get you to a doctor."

She nodded and turned in a slow circle, taking in their location. Though they stood on a relatively safe spot, the whitewater river bordered one side of their patch of beach and rock walls made up the other three. Without a raft, the river wasn't an option for departure.

That left rock climbing. The very thought of scaling the cliff made her tired, but there seemed little choice. "No time like the present," she said, heading toward the cliff.

Angel grabbed her arm before she took two steps. "You might have a concussion."

Concussion or not, she had to get out of there if she wanted to live. And that was the plan. She'd been through too much to give in now. And this time, not even Angel could save her. She had to save herself.

Or at least climb a cliff. She glanced up. "Let's go with this side. It's lower, and with the jutting rocks it might have better handholds. Besides, how hard can it be?"

"Famous last words," Angel said. "Usually followed by something that is a helluva lot harder than anyone thought."

"Do we really have a choice?" Fiona asked.

"We can wait."

"For what? For the gangsters to return? For a ladder to fall out of the sky? For my head to explode?" Her headache grew with her anger, making her eyes water and her temper short. Perhaps there wasn't anything to be done for a concussion, but she'd climb a mountain for an aspirin.

She continued, "You said it yourself: I need a doctor."

Angel looked at her, the cliff, then back to her.

"Let me help you."

She raised a brow. "What are you going to do? Carry me?" she asked, not caring that her voice was sharp. "The sooner we do this the sooner I can get some ibuprofen."

He let go of her arm, and she wiped at her eyes. He glared at her, but if she hadn't known better she would have said he was worried.

She pressed a finger against her forehead, feeling like a bitch. "Sorry."

He gave her a tight nod. "You go first. Take your time, and if you feel at all like you might pass out or fall, you call out."

"I will," she replied, grateful he didn't insist on arguing with her. They walked over to the base of the cliff. She'd thought it was twenty feet, but from this angle it looked like it went up forever.

"Remember, this is not a race," Angel said. "Watch your foot placement." He cupped his hands. She didn't argue but stepped onto them. "Hang on." Shifting his hands until his palm rested against her sole, she kept her balance by hugging the wall as he boosted her upward.

Halfway there already.

She grabbed a rock just above her head and searched for a toehold. "I'm good," she called over her shoulder.

Angel let go of her foot, and her body trembled as she found herself supporting her weight. Black spots danced in front of her eyes, clouding her vision and making her regret her earlier bravado.

She remembered her father telling her, after a date had ended badly and she was questioning her own actions, that there was no going back. There was only forward.

Good advice that transcended a situation of the heart to the more physical.

She had to go forward. If she gave up, who knew what would happen. Angel might think the gang wouldn't come after them but she wasn't as sure. And the thought of being trapped on the tiny beach and subject to anyone's whim made her shake harder than any physical feat of strength.

"Fiona?" Angel asked. She heard the multitude of questions beneath her name. Was she going to pass out? Could she climb two feet, much less twenty? Was he going to have to save her? *Again?*

No. For once, she was saving herself.

"Let's get out of here." Reaching upward, she found a handhold and began to climb.

Angel kept an eye on Fiona as she climbed. Twice she faltered. But both times she recovered, maintained her grip and moved upward.

Damn. Scaling a cliff with a pounding headache took more than strength of body. It took strength of will.

A third falter later, she reached the top and disappeared over the edge. He was right behind her and, with a grunt, pulled himself up and fell to the ground, exhausted.

Fiona lay on her back next to him, her breathing heavy and her eyes closed. A sheen of sweat covered her body. "Are you going to pass out?" he asked.

"Not right now," she replied. "Perhaps later."

"Just let me know." He chuckled, taking a moment to enjoy the sensation of being prone in relative safety. It had been a long, painful morning and the physical and emotional stress was taking its toll on them both.

"I'll see what I can do," Fiona said. Already, her breathing was slowing to normal. She sighed, a familiar sound that told him she was falling asleep.

He'd always heard that people with concussions weren't supposed to sleep, but he couldn't remember if that was an old wives' tale or if it was fact. When he'd gone into the field, he'd hired a medic. His knowledge was limited to the more obvious problems—like bullet wounds.

Not useful in this situation.

He couldn't take the chance on what might be fact and what might be fiction. "Wake up," he said, giving her shoulder a little push.

"I'm awake," she murmured.

"Like hell." He sat up and shook her. "Get. Up."

"Bite. Me." Her eyelids fluttered, and she gazed at him with smiling blue eyes. God, she was beautiful.

And right now, she reminded him of Isabel. It wasn't her physical appearance so much but the combination of trust and mischief that lit her from within.

Trust was a responsibility that weighed on his shoulders. The mischief? Well, that made him want to kiss her. Again. Hard. But that would have to wait until he knew she was safe. "Either move," he said, rising to stand over her. "Or I'll carry you."

Her eyes widened with surprise then narrowed with annoyance. "I don't think so."

Pride. Another trait she and Isabel shared.

Despite the similarities, she wasn't Isabel. Fiona was less impulsive. Her temper was more controlled. Isabel would have never simply jumped into the water. She'd have argued about what to do until the gang dragged her up the cliff. Then she'd have argued with *them*.

As for right now, Isabel would lie there and make him pick her up—possibly biting him or kissing him. Probably both.

God, he missed her, and he knew a part of him always would. But the pain of her loss was fading.

And it was because of Fiona. Hell, he hadn't had so much as a nightmare since she walked into Tierra Roja. She needed him then, and she needed him now. Somehow, that was healing him.

He wasn't sure how or why, but he knew one thing. He had to follow through with his promise to help her, even if it meant braving her temper.

Squatting next to Fiona, he met her annoyed gaze. "Do you really want to test me?"

She shoved him away and tottered to her feet with a groan. "Okay, I'm up. Now what?"

He gestured downstream. "Let's move."

Chapter 9

"We're in luck," Angel said, taking Fiona's arm as they skirted the edge of a rock formation. They'd been walking for about an hour and while her headache had subsided, she wasn't sure how much farther she could force her weary body along. The foliage along the river had thinned, which made their trek easier, but it was still rough going due to the steep terrain.

More than once, Angel had offered to carry her and had even gone so far as to try and pick her up, but she'd refused. She'd come this far; she'd go farther.

"What is it?" she asked, her voice hoarse.

"Down there. A village."

She squinted into the bright sunlight and finally made out the quasi-straight lines of structures.

She almost cried in relief.

Instead, her legs buckled, and she fell to the ground. Dirt and rock dug into her palms, making her wince.

"Fiona!" Angel dropped beside her.

"I'm fine," she said, waving him off. She was more embarrassed than hurt, but she wasn't about to tell him.

"Here, let me." He took her hand in his, his touch light and sure as he dusted off the dirt to survey the damage.

"A little scrape," he said. "You probably got worse from the river."

"Compared to the past twenty-four hours, a scrape just doesn't seem like a big deal," she said with a smile.

"Glad to see you're keeping a sense of humor," Angel said.

Fiona glanced past him to the village below. Though a distance away, she made out a few people. "So, what do we do? Go around or go in?"

Angel hesitated. "We go around if we have to, but I'd rather get help. We're not going to last much longer out here otherwise."

No, *she* wouldn't last much longer. He'd be fine, and they both knew it. Still, it was kind of him to say so.

"Wait until dark?" she asked.

Again, Angel hesitated. "It's siesta. I can go now with little chance of detection."

"Are you sure?" Even as she asked, she knew it was a foolish question.

They'd been chased by bandits, there was a bounty on their heads, and she carried a tape that could put Montoya in jail. No place could be considered safe, and the thought of Angel approaching an unknown village in daylight made her shiver despite the heat of the day.

But the thought of sleeping in a real bed made her ache with longing.

Angel nodded. "I'm a trained professional, remember?"

"I know," she said, holding on to that thought.

"Good. Stay here and don't call attention to yourself." He rose but hunkered low. "I'll be back soon."

What if he wasn't? What if the peaceful village was anything but that? The thought of losing Angel, of being left alone, was unnerving. She grabbed his hand. "Promise me you'll come back."

His gaze softened, and he squeezed her fingers. "I promise."

Reluctantly, she let go then watched him make his way to the village until she lost sight of him in the scrub and the trees.

Carefully, Fiona lay back against one of the boulders, hugged herself, watched the insects dart around her, and tried not to think of what would happen to her, to Angel, if he were caught.

A branch cracked nearby. Fiona stiffened but didn't move. Cautiously, she rose to her knees and turned her attention back to the village, squinting for a better view. It had been at least an hour since Angel left and there was still no sign of his return. "He should be back by now," she muttered.

Picking up a stone, she rolled it between her hands and told herself that she wouldn't panic.

At least not yet.

A hand touched her foot and she yelped, dropping the stone as she tried to get away.

"It's me," Angel said, his voice next to her shoulder.

Fiona whacked him on the arm. "You scared the hell out of me," she said, whacking him again but not meaning it.

He laughed. "Sorry."

She doubted it.

He continued, "But you'll forgive me when I tell you that the village is safe. Or as safe as we can get in Colombia."

"Are you sure?" she asked. It was about time they had a little luck.

"It's a little weird," Angel admitted. "There's something going on down there, but I don't think they're bandits."

"Drugs?" Fiona asked.

"I don't think so," Angel said. "Otherwise, the villagers would be dirt-poor and beaten. They're not."

"I trust your judgment," she said.

"Thanks." Unexpectedly, Angel kissed the top of her head. Unlike their previous kisses, this one didn't make her tremble. It was comforting. Familiar. Like a kiss from someone she'd known forever.

And unsettling, she realized. Lust she understood, and with a man like Angel in close proximity, lust was expected.

But this sense of intimacy disturbed her.

"Let's go," he said. Taking her hand, he helped her to her feet.

Carefully, they made their way down the rocky hill toward the small adobe houses.

They reached the village, and a chorus of barking dogs began. The few people on the dirt road stopped and stared. Curtains opened then quickly slid shut.

No one said a word.

"This was a bad idea," Fiona said, trying to ignore the suspicious glances. "It's not as if my head will explode if I don't get aspirin. We should go."

"It'll be fine," Angel replied. "Besides, you're getting paler each minute."

And weaker, she thought, but she didn't want to acknowledge the fact aloud. "Do not make this all about me," Fiona said.

"I'm not. I'm stating the facts. You need rest, food and water."

She hated it when he was right. "Do you really think they'll help us?" Fiona asked, licking her lips at the thought of water.

"I hope so."

"So who do we ask for help?"

"Over here," Angel said, pointing ahead of them.

At the end of the road was an adobe fortress and, peeking over the top of the wall, the tile roof of a house. "Whoever lives there is the town *patrón*."

Or head drug lord, Fiona thought. "What about a doctor?"

"If he's the patriarch of the village, and I think he is, he'll get us access with few questions asked. If there isn't a doctor, then the *patrón* should have medicine. I hope."

It made sense. Start with the wealthiest. Besides, they didn't have much of a choice unless they wanted to spend the night sleeping outside, and last night's experience was enough to last her for quite awhile.

"What are we going to tell him? We can't tell him the truth."

"That we were rafting down the river and wrecked. It's not too far from the truth."

"It'll do," Fiona agreed. A movement in her peripheral vision caught her attention, and she turned her head in time to see a shadow dart between the buildings. "We're being followed," she whispered.

"I know," Angel said. "I doubt they get many visitors here."

Despite the blasé tone, Fiona noticed that his pace increased. In less than a minute, they stood outside the walls of the affluent house. A rope hung alongside the heavy wooden gate and, at the top, a bell. Angel tugged the rope, and the sound of the bell resonated through the night air.

They waited for a minute but received no answer. Angel pulled the rope again and an elderly man opened the door. Dressed in black slacks and a white linen shirt, he stood out against the red adobe walls and floor. And though his hair was white and his skin wrinkled, Fiona saw the handsome man beneath the age.

"*Buenos noches. ¿En que le puedo ayudar?*"

It was a good start.

"*Buenos noches, señor. Hemos tenido un accidente,*" Angel explained.

They'd had an accident? That was an understatement. Apparently, the man thought so, as well. He shook his head at her, probably disturbed that she looked like something the cat dragged in.

He stood aside so they could enter. *"Soy Don Marcos. Por favor, pasan."*

Before Fiona could protest, Angel scooped her into his arms and carried her across the threshold. Don Marcos shut the gate behind them then edged past and gestured for them to follow.

Still in Angel's arms, Fiona took in their surroundings. *Patrón* or drug dealer, this man lived well. They walked along a brick path bordered by a line of trees and exotic flowers, like birds-of-paradise. At the end of the path was a home constructed from hand-crafted adobe. They crossed the threshold and Fiona's jaw dropped.

The main room was a combination of extravagance and local goods. A heavy woolen blanket of native design was slung across the back of a couch covered in raw silk the color of eggplant. Oak bookcases filled with classics lined the walls and every inch of bare shelf space was occupied with a native trinket.

"Magnífico," Angel muttered under his breath,

Don Marcos tossed a few pillows off the couch to make space for Fiona. Angel set her down, and she sank into the cushions.

A short woman with long, braided hair walked into the room carrying two large glasses of water. Smiling, she handed them to Angel and Fiona. Fiona raised the glass to her mouth and let the cool water slide down her throat.

When she set the glass down, it was empty. "This is heaven," she groaned.

Angel grinned at her. "Glad to see you smile."

Fiona flushed, embarrassed she was that transparent in her enjoyment. He'd been through as much as she, and he sipped his water, unconcerned.

"It's okay. You've earned it." His smile broadened. Leaning over, he spoke low. "Let me do the talking. I suspect Don Marcos is a traditionalist and that means you keep silent unless spoken to."

So much for equal rights, Fiona thought. But this was not her country and her traditions. "Of course."

Angel turned to talk to their host, and though her Spanish was excellent, it was no match for the men's rapid-fire conversation. In less than a minute, Fiona tuned them out. On the teak table next to the couch was a chess set. She picked up one of the carved pieces and recognized the glasslike finish of obsidian. She turned it in the light and it reflected a rainbow.

A flash of movement caught her eye, and she spotted another servant watching them. Apparently she and Angel were quite the entertainment.

"Ella puede dormir abajo del pasillo. Usted dormirá en este lado."

Like hearing her name at a cocktail party, Don Marco's words cut through the hubbub of her mind. Fiona turned her attention back to the men.

Don Marcos was going to put them in separate rooms? Split them up for the night? Her heart thumped hard inside her chest. She didn't know Don Marcos. The people. The village. What if Montoya or the bandits found them?

Her imagination kicked into overdrive, and she imagined Don Marcos and his men coming to her room. Kidnapping her and demanding ransom. Perhaps giving her to revolutionaries. Or even selling her to a rich drug lord where she'd live a life of servitude.

She grabbed Angel's hand. "No," she said. She could not be separated from Angel. Not here. Not until they were safe in the States.

"Usted ar no casado. Es inadecuado," Don Marcos said.

He was splitting them up because they weren't married? Angel turned to her. "It'll be okay," he said, and an expression flashed across his face that she'd never seen and wasn't sure she could place.

Fear? Uncertainty? Whatever it was, it wasn't good and only added to her panic. Her heart beat harder, and she tightened her hold on Angel's hand.

"Estamos casados," Angel said.

We're married?

Don Marcos glanced at Fiona's bare left hand.

"Lo perdí," she said, hoping he believed her claim of losing it.

He raised a brow and shook his head, *"Pardón, pero—"*

Angel continued, *"No querida, yo lo tengo."* He turned back to Don Marcos. *"Se golpea la cabeza con una piedra y se queda confundida."*

Oh hell. What was Angel thinking? He had the ring?

He has a plan, Fiona told herself. Still, her stomach did a flip worthy of an Olympic champion.

Angel kneeled down, pulled her hand to his mouth, and kissed her ring finger. "Play along," he whispered so lightly she almost missed it.

He raised his head. The *look,* the one she couldn't place, flashed over his features again.

Letting her go, he unzipped one of the side pockets on his cargo pants, reached inside and pulled out a silver band. He held it out to her, and Fiona's eyes widened.

It was a wedding band.

"Take it," Angel whispered.

But she couldn't. She didn't know what to think or do or say. She could only stare at the silver circle Angel held between his fingers. Where the hell had that come from?

And why did he carry it?

"Damn it," Angel muttered. Taking Fiona's left hand in his, he slid it onto her ring finger.

"Mil disculpas." Don Marcos smiled and nodded.

"No hay problema," Angel replied.

Finally pulling her gaze away from the wedding band that adorned her finger, Fiona met Angel's hot gaze and placed the look—the one she hadn't recognized earlier. It wasn't fear. Or uncertainty. Or anything so simple.

It was grief.

* * *

God help him, he'd screwed up, Angel thought as he and Fiona followed Don Marcos down the hallway to the bedroom that would be theirs.

And it wasn't just a minor, "Let me write a check to cover the cost" screw-up. No. This was big. Awkward.

He hadn't planned to offer her Isabel's ring. Given a choice, she'd never have known he carried it, but she was pale and tired, and he might not admit it aloud, but he was worried about her. So, he'd acted on impulse to help her. Now, there was no taking it back.

Worse, as soon as they were alone, she'd want an explanation, and there was no getting around it.

Don Marcos stopped at the end of the hallway and opened the door. The room on the other side of the threshold was simple, with a queen-size bed, a dresser, few chairs and a large mirror. Despite its minimalism, Angel bet there were thousand-count sheets on the bed and that the dresser was mahogany.

A pale yellow blouse and long, rose-pink skirt were laid out across the bed. Next to them, a large, mesh bag.

One of the servants hustled into the room and left another stack of clothes next to Fiona's then hurried out.

Clothes for him, he realized. Though his new clothes were more practical than Fiona's. Made from rough cotton, the dark trousers and blue cotton shirt were crafted to last a lifetime.

Don Marcos gestured toward a closed door on the far side of the room. *"Hay toallas en el cuarto de baño,"*

"Gracias," Fiona replied. *"Un baño será agradable "*

Saying that a shower was welcome was an understatement.

"La cena esto en una hora," Don Marcos said, giving them a brief nod.

They had an hour before dinner? Plenty of time for him and Fiona to talk. *Great.*

"Gracias," Angel replied and closed the door.

Taking a deep breath, he turned around, leaned with his back against the wood and waited for Fiona to speak.

She didn't say a word. Didn't glance at her beringed hand. Didn't even cast him a quick glance. She simply crossed the room and sat on the bed.

He'd worried what she might say. Dreaded it. Prepared explanations and run scenarios through his head to create a response to every question she might ask.

Now he'd give a year's pay to hear her say anything. Crossing the room, he sat beside her.

She ran a hand over the skirt. "Where am I supposed to hide a gun?"

"I don't think women carry weapons in Don Marcos's world," Angel said, grateful for any conversation.

"Well, women in his world don't get shot at on a daily basis," she said.

"True," he agreed, dragging out the word and wondering where the conversation was headed.

"It's nice of him," she said, picking up the blouse and holding it against her torso.

"Nice has nothing to do with it," Angel replied, the mundane topic both comforting and dreadful—like the silence before a hail of bullets. "It's his duty to help us, since no one else in the village can afford to take us in."

"I am sure our marriage helped," Fiona said, folding the blouse back up and setting it on the bedspread.

Angel stiffened. Was this the fight?

But he realized there was no sarcasm beneath the words. In fact, her voice was flat as she stared at him. Waiting.

God help him, he'd rather face a barrage of bullets than Fiona's silent, accusing gaze. "You must have questions," Angel said, unable to take the tense quiet.

"Just one."

"What?"

"What happened to her?" There was no doubt that she knew the answer—there was only one—still, she demanded he speak.

He didn't want to. But it was her business now as well as his. He'd made sure of that. Angel ran his hands through his hair. "She died." Short. To the point. And truthful, but only on the surface. There was so much more to what happened.

"You were married?"

He thought he detected anger in her tone but wasn't sure. He shook his head. "No. She wanted to elope but I refused."

Then he found himself wanting to speak. "I wanted the production. To see her in the white dress walking down the aisle. To me," he said. The words spilled from his mouth, refusing to remain still and silent in his head now that he'd begun his story.

He clenched his hands into tight fists. "But there was no wedding. No honeymoon. No houseful of kids. No growing old together."

There was only death. Grief. And a final goodbye as the undertaker lowered Isabel's coffin into the ground. To add to the pain, her family blamed him for Isabel's death, refusing to even bury her with her ring.

Fiona held her hand up, and the ring glinted in the dim light. She stared at it and Angel wondered what was going through her thoughts. Was she angry? Did she hate him? What?

Finally, she placed her hand back in her lap. "Why do you carry it?"

Angel sighed. "Complicated question."

"Try."

Her request was fair. Isabel was gone. Why carry around a ring she never wore? "I didn't know what else to do with it," he replied. "The thought of selling it seemed wrong. It's not as if I could wear it. And I couldn't leave it in my apartment. What if I were robbed?"

"So you carry it in your pocket."

"Yes." Like a talisman or charm or a memory of what might have been, he couldn't let go of the white-gold band. So he'd carried it until he placed it on Fiona's finger.

"That's not so complicated," Fiona said, her voice tinged with irony.

"I guess not," Angel said.

"Still, it feels odd." She twisted the ring. "But probably more so for you than me, I'd guess."

"Odd is an understatement," Angel replied. It was beyond odd. It was disconcerting as hell and, though Isabel was gone, seeing her ring on Fiona's hand felt like a betrayal.

"I appreciate your letting me wear it," Fiona said. "I hated the thought of us being separated. What if something happened?"

"My thoughts, as well," Angel said.

Fiona put her hands back on her lap. "Can I ask you something?"

He nodded.

"What was her name?"

He hadn't spoken her name in over a year—ever since he arrived in Bogotá and decided to drink his life away. "Isabel."

"Isabel."

There was no jealousy in Fiona's tone. She spoke Isabel's name as if it belonged to a friend. Someone she cared for. He was surprised to feel her hand slip into his. "You miss her, don't you?" she asked.

He thought about the question. "Yes, but more than that, I miss what might have been," he replied.

Her hand still in his. "Thanks."

"For what?"

"For telling me the truth. For telling me about Isabel. For, well, everything."

He believed her. "You're welcome."

* * *

"How do I look?" Fiona asked. She'd taken her new clothes into the bathroom to change after her shower, and while a skirt wasn't practical, it felt amazing to be clean.

"Do you really want to ask a guy that question?" Angel asked.

"Point taken." Fiona stopped midtwirl and tossed him a towel. "It's all yours."

It was weird, in a good but unexpected way, that they could joke already.

Angel grabbed the towel in midair, but before he took a step toward the shower, there was a pounding on the door.

Carefully, Angel opened it. Don Marcos stood in the entry. *"¡Rápido! ¡Rápido de prisa!"*

"What is it?" Fiona asked.

"They are coming." Don Marcos hurried into the room and held out a piece of paper. He spoke English? Somehow that didn't surprise her. Nor did his hiding it from her and Angel until now. Don Marcos wasn't the type of man to give away a potential advantage. Which made his sudden revelation somehow more frightening. Angel took the flyer, frowned then handed it to Fiona.

On it were pictures of both herself and Angel. Underneath was a list of their crimes and the monetary reward for their capture.

"Montoya?" Angel asked what they both knew.

"Sí," Don Marcos replied

"Dammit to hell," Fiona swore, not missing the fact that Don Marcos made a *tsk*ing sound at her swearing. She didn't care.

The memory of Montoya chilled her. No smile. No frown. No expression at all as he gunned down Maria.

And Tony.

She couldn't forget Tony.

Fiona took a deep breath, forcing herself to remain calm. "Who told him?" she asked, crumpling up the flyer in her fist then dropping it to the ground.

"None of my people," Don Marcos replied. "They are loyal."

"Then how did they find us so fast?"

"Did anyone else see you?" Don Marcos asked. "Anyone?"

"Bandits," Angel said. "We were chased. It's how we ended up in the river."

"And we are the closest village," Don Marcos said.

"What now?" she asked.

"I have no love for Montoya," Don Marcos explained. "But you must leave before he arrives."

"How will he even know we are here?" Fiona asked, grasping at hope. "Can't we hide?"

"He will search every house. Even mine," Don Marcos said. "If he finds you here it will put my people in danger. You must go. Now."

"How?" Angel asked.

"My driver will take you someplace safe where you can continue your journey."

"Thank you for your generosity," Angel said.

"You're welcome," Don Marcos replied. "Now come. It is time to go."

It was always time to go. The thought made Fiona want to cry. Instead, she rolled her pants into a ball, keeping the tape inside. Stuffing the wad of cloth into the mesh bag, she hurried after the men.

She wasn't sure what to expect from a man like Don Marcos, especially considering the location of his compound. A jeep, perhaps? A Volkswagen? Something old and well used but serviceable.

She didn't expect a silver Mercedes convertible with one of the villagers behind the wheel.

"Nice car," Angel said, hurrying to the passenger's side.

"Thank you." Don Marcos tossed the driver the keys.

A petite woman, dressed in a simple blue skirt and white

blouse, appeared as if out of nowhere and handed Fiona a basket of food. "Thank you," Fiona said, putting the basket into the backseat.

Don Marcos looked to Angel. "Be careful with her."

Fiona slid onto the leather seat, wondering if he meant her or the car.

"Of course," Angel said.

Their host smiled. "Come back when you have more time. I am sure you have an interesting story."

"We'll come back," Fiona said, taking a seat. "I think you have an interesting story, as well."

Don Marcos laughed. "Of course." Then he leaned against the door, all laughter gone. "I am not sure where you are heading, and I do not want to know. So, I have instructed my driver to drop you off at the top of the pass. From there, you should be safe as long as you keep out of sight and don't take foolish chances."

He leaned in. "If you are so inclined, follow the river into the mountains until you see a bridge. Cross it and follow the river. But be careful. There are many natives in the mountains and not all are friendly."

"Got it." Angel signaled the driver to start the car.

"Don Marcos?" Fiona said, her reporter's curiosity kicking in.

"Yes?"

"Why are you helping us? There's a reward."

Don Marcos grinned. "Montoya confiscated my plane and took my cargo." Whatever the cargo was, she was sure it wasn't wooden dolls.

"You are not afraid of him?" she asked. "What he'll do to you if he finds you gave us shelter?"

"No. He does not scare me."

"Not even to find us?" Angel asked.

Don Marcos grinned. "I am what you call godfather to Jose Ramirez."

"The president of Colombia?" Fiona asked, stunned.

Don Marcos nodded. "He is a good man. Bad decisions at times, but a good man."

Bad decisions. Like making Montoya head of security for Colombia. That was more than bad, but she wasn't going to argue the point. Not now.

But the relationship explained the wealth, and why he was safe from Montoya. It could also explain why Don Marcos was allowed to operate as a drug lord with no repercussions.

"We should go," Angel said.

Fiona kissed Don Marcos on the cheek, liking him despite his profession. It was hard to condemn him when he was obviously using his money to help his people.

Besides, as a reporter, it wasn't her job to judge Don Marcos. Especially when she didn't know his full story. "Thank you."

He patted her hand. "You are welcome." He scooted around the front of the car and pushed on the large hinged door but stopped when it was only a few inches open.

"What's wrong?" Even as she asked the question, the hairs on the back of her neck rose, making her shiver.

Don Marcos peeked through the small opening. "We are too late. Montoya is here."

Chapter 10

Angel left the engine running. "How many?"

"One jeep. Two covered trucks," Don Marcos replied, his tone stronger, sterner, giving Angel a glimpse of the steel beneath the polite, unassuming surface. "Two men in the front of each. Probably more in the back of the trucks, but they're covered so there is no way to count."

An accurate count didn't matter. The initial numbers were enough to nix the idea of trying to leave through the front door. And trying to outrun Montoya wasn't any better. The Mercedes was certainly faster, but once they encountered rough terrain, Montoya would catch them. He and Fiona would have to sneak out, make their way to the woods and lie low until it was safe to move. "Do you have a back door?"

Don Marcos nodded.

Shouting caught Angel's attention. Montoya himself was

questioning one of the villagers. He must be frantic to find them to be doing some of the dirty work.

The man denied any knowledge of either Angel or Fiona.

Then there was shouting. A slap and a scream. Stay strong, Angel thought.

More demands, then Angel heard the phrase *dos extranjeros—two strangers*—and knew that sneaking away was no longer an option.

"Estúpido," Don Marcos hissed the word. His lips pressed in anger, he turned to Angel. "I hoped it would not come to this, but there is a tunnel that comes out a few houses away. It also contains a weapons cache."

Finally, a break. He might not have agreed with Don Marcos's occupation, but at this moment he was glad the old man was both prepared and paranoid.

"We're going to shoot our way out?" Fiona asked.

"No, *we're* not," Angel replied.

Fiona frowned. "Excuse me?" She crossed her arms over her chest and flashed him a defiant glare that he'd come to know a little too well.

He didn't have time for a confrontation. A week ago, he'd have told her to shut up and let him do his job. Not that it would work. Call it reporter's curiosity or just Fiona being Fiona, but she always seemed to need an explanation.

"You are going to wait here. *I* am going to go down the tunnel and deal with the problem."

She didn't appear convinced that the plan would work. Hell, neither was he, but that didn't matter. "And I'm supposed to sit here while you take on an army," she said.

"Yes."

She raised a dark brow. "No."

"Fiona, I don't have time to argue—"

"You never do. Yet here we are. Again. Arguing."

Angel looked at Don Marcos. "I need to deal with this while they're all together. Once they start breaking down doors, they'll be spread out and it'll be too late to contain the issue."

"He is right, *señora*," Don Marcos said. "I have a safe place for you to wait."

"Then we can both wait there."

"Not happening," Angel said, frustrated with Fiona's tenacity. "They know we're here and they won't stop searching until they find us."

Fiona's brows knit together. "I'm going."

Angel tensed. What the hell was wrong with him that he always ended up with women who had more stubbornness than sense?

Voices outside grew louder. Damn it, they'd already wasted more time than they had. "You'll do exactly as I say," he said, agreeing despite his better judgment. "Understood?"

"Yes."

He wasn't sure if she was pleased at the victory. If she was, she had the sense to hide it.

"*Señor*, this isn't a good idea," Don Marcos said. He took Fiona's arm as she stepped out of the car to follow Angel.

"Do you want to try and stop her?" Angel asked.

Don Marcos shook his head, a smile curling his mouth. "She is a strong one, no?"

"Yes," Angel agreed, both hating and loving that about Fiona. Fiona smiled.

"And stubborn as a burro," Angel finished. Outside, a car door slammed.

The smile turned into a glare. "Let's do this," she said.

"Follow Anna," Don Marcos said. "She will show you where to go."

"What about you?" Angel asked. "You won't be safe." The old man might be the godfather to the president, but Angel wasn't sure it was enough to keep him alive now.

"Montoya will complain. Threaten. But he will do nothing as long as he doesn't find you."

"You're sure?" Fiona asked. Angel knew she carried the same worries. She'd seen too much death, all dealt by Montoya.

"I am confident." Don Marcos patted her hand. "Do not assume that everyone in my village is a farmer."

No doubt there.

Anna beckoned to them. "Go," Don Marcos urged them. "Go with God."

"Thank you," Angel said, taking Fiona's hand.

She held back for a second, kissing the old man on the cheek. "Be careful."

Quickly, they followed Anna down the hallway and into what Angel assumed was Don Marcos's bedroom. She opened the wardrobe. It was full of clothes that ranged from Armani suits to old, dirt-stained slacks. Shoes lined the bottom.

Anna pushed aside the clothes and shoes, and pressed a knob on the side. A hidden hatch on the bottom of the wardrobe fell open.

The maid fished around inside the wardrobe and, after a few seconds, handed Angel a flashlight. *"Prisa. Prisa."*

There was no need to tell him to hurry.

"Go." Angel stood aside, handing the flashlight to Fiona. She didn't hesitate but took the light and lowered herself onto the ladder and into the tunnel. Angel watched her climb down. When she reached twenty feet, she waved for him to follow.

It was a helluva deep tunnel for escape, but there wasn't time to ask questions. He climbed onto the rickety ladder, taking a moment to shut the trap door above his head before he descended.

The air smelled of earth and sweat, and grew cooler with each foot downward. He reached the bottom and it was almost chilly.

"Angel, I don't know what this guy does, but I don't think he's a drug lord."

Angel turned his attention to where she shone the light. What

Don Marcos called a getaway tunnel was a mine. The walls were scarred with recent digging and picks lay scattered on the ground and propped against the earthen walls.

"What do you think they're looking for?" Fiona asked. "Gold?"

"Colombia isn't known for its gold," Angel replied. He peered at one of the areas that looked as if it were subject to recent activity. Something shiny and green caught his eyes, and he pulled it from the wall. "What we are known for are emeralds," he said, holding up the small cluster of stone. Though uncut, the crystals glimmered in the light.

"What?" Fiona's eyes widened.

"Emeralds. That's where he gets his money. That's what he's hiding from Montoya. Or trying to." He handed the stones to Fiona. Her jaw dropped.

"They're stunning."

"And in this case useless, unless we plan to use them to brain Montoya," Angel said, pushing past her to a pile of stacked boxes pushed against the wall. He opened one. M-16s.

He took two. Checking that the clips were full he handed one to Fiona, plus an extra clip from another box. "Think you can handle this?" he asked.

"Shoot and spray?"

"Close," he said. "This is a semiautomatic. You'll get three-round bursts. Keep your eye on the target. Don't take your finger off the trigger."

She let the emeralds fall to the dirt and took the weapon, her hands shaking.

"You sure you want to do this?" he asked. The gun trembled despite her white-knuckled grip on the butt.

"I'm sure."

He wasn't going to argue but he still didn't like it. She wasn't like him. She wasn't a killer. And he didn't want her to be.

He opened up the last crate. It was stocked with M-203s—

grenade launchers that fit onto the M-16s—plus ammunition. He whistled in surprise. Don Marcos was prepared for war.

Then again, this was Colombia.

He fit one of the M203s onto his weapon.

"What's that?" Fiona asked.

"Grenade launcher," Angel replied.

"Do I get one?" she asked, her tone both uncertain and excited.

"No," he said. The last thing he wanted was grenades in the hand of an amateur.

She opened her mouth in what he was sure was the beginning of an argument.

"You said you'd do what I say." Angel cut her off with the reminder. "No argument."

Fiona snapped her jaw shut. "So I did."

He gave a nod of approval. "Follow me."

"Of course."

Fiona hefted the weapon, which was surprisingly light, and hurried after Angel, knowing this was the most insane thing she'd ever done. But the thought of letting him go at Montoya alone was more unbearable.

She knew what that monster was capable of, and she'd be damned if Angel was going to wade into the fray without someone guarding his back. She might not be much in the way of backup, but she was better than nothing.

Or so she kept telling the little voice in her head that insisted she was a hindrance.

A glint of green caught her eye. A thick vein of stone—some emeralds and some kind of clear quartz—ran along the wall at eye level. *Emeralds.* Who would have thought? Well, Don Marcos's secret was safe with her. She owed the man.

She and Angel went about forty feet, turned a corner, and the tunnel came to an abrupt halt at another ladder. This was it.

Fiona took a deep breath. Angel hung his weapon over his shoulder, pulled out his handgun and climbed upward. She followed, and a chill that had nothing to do with temperature crept up her spine.

Angel looked down at her, finger over his lips, signaling her to be quiet. He counted with his fingers. *One. Two. Three.*

Fiona tensed, held her breath, and he pushed open the hatch above them. Gun at arm's length, he popped upward and into the room.

"Clear," he said, climbing out.

Fiona followed. They'd entered an empty shed. No, she realized as she looked around the room. Not a shed. The villagers had disguised the tunnel to the mine as a relatively large outhouse.

She chuckled despite the impending chaos. Angel was already at the door, waiting. He thumbed the latch, hesitated. "You still sure?" he asked again.

She couldn't blame his trepidation. She was a novice with shaky hands. "As much as I can be," she admitted.

"Good enough." He pushed open the door, taking stock of the area. "Stay close."

Cautiously, they scooted around the shed. A movement caught Fiona's eye, sending her heart racing, but Angel was already turning, gun raised.

In the glassless window of the nearest home, Fiona caught a flash of crisp, yellow blouse and long dark hair before the figure disappeared. One of the villagers, she realized, willing her pulse to slow.

Angel motioned her to follow. Moving as fast as they dared, they stuck to the shadows of the shabby building. Voices drifted on the air, and Angel held up his hand, signaling her to stop. Fiona crouched in the dirt, her back pressed to the hut behind her.

She cocked her head to listen. A male voice asked about them. Where were they? Denial that they'd ever arrived was the reply. She recognized the second voice: Don Marcos.

Angel pulled her close, his mouth against her ear. "I'm going to make my way to the back of the trucks and do some damage. You wait here. When it's safe, I'll call for you."

Though he met her worry with confidence, Fiona's blood chilled. "What kind of damage?"

Angel smiled. "Let's just say that things will go boom."

She eyed the grenade launcher, still unsure. "There's a lot of men out there and only one of you."

He shrugged. "I handled the ambush at the television station, I can handle this. They're trained but I'm better."

Though he told the truth, it felt wrong to let him take that kind of chance while she waited in safety. "I can help you," she whispered.

"No, you'll distract me and get me killed. Is that what you want?"

The words were as painful as a slap across the face and she stiffened. "Of course not, but—"

"This isn't up for debate." Angel interrupted her. "I have to go before the villagers come out. I don't want collateral damage." He leaned in and kissed her, his mouth hard on hers. "Be careful," Angel said. "Be careful and keep an eye on your surroundings."

He left her behind. Fiona wiped a sweaty palm on her pants and Isabel's ring flashed in the sunlight. Quickly, she thrust it into her pocket. Not that it would catch much attention in her current location, but she wasn't taking any chances when Angel's life hung in the balance.

Silently, she counted her heartbeats, waiting for gunfire. Shouts. Anything besides mumbled chatter punctuated with silence.

An explosion ripped the air followed by screams and cries of panic. Perhaps of pain. Fiona leapt to her feet. Remaining wary, she hurried to the side of Don Marcos's hacienda, peeking around the corner.

Chaos met her gaze. Thick black smoke from a burning truck filled the air. Don Marcos wasn't in sight, and neither were any villagers. Soldiers dressed in green fatigues crouched in the acrid air, eyes cutting back and forth, searching for the enemy and finding nothing but confusion.

She didn't see Montoya, but more important, she didn't see Angel.

Motion inside the dark cloud caught her attention, and she squinted, willing her eyes to adjust. *Tall. Dark hair.*

Angel?

A breeze rolled the smoke toward her, and she coughed. The figure turned toward her, clearing the cloud.

Not Angel. *Montoya.*

His eyes met hers. He smiled. She recognized the grin of satisfaction and triumph, and she knew the truth. That he'd won again. Taken someone she loved.

Taken Angel.

She clutched her chest as a sudden, sharp pain drove her to her knees. "Angel."

Black-booted feet entered her field of vision, drawing her gaze upward, past fatigue-covered legs, leather belt, tan shirt and once again to Montoya's smile. He held out his hand. "Ms. Macmillan, you have something for me?" he said in English.

He acted as if the tape belonged to him. Blinding anger roared to life inside Fiona, blotting out the pain in her heart. This wasn't right. Wasn't fair. She would not let him win. Not without a fight.

Deliberately, she brushed ashes off her cheek. "Screw you." She ground the words out through her clenched jaw.

His eyes narrowed. *"Puta."* He raised his gun.

The sounds of chaos faded. Light faded. Nothing touched her. She looked into the open end of Montoya's gun. She knew she was dead, and she didn't care.

* * *

His T-shirt pulled up over his mouth so he could breathe, Angel worked his way through the smoke, keeping low and watching for an ambush.

A groan caught his attention, and he crawled toward it. One of Montoya's men lay on the ground. A piece of shrapnel over six inches long poked out of his thigh, and his right arm was covered with second-degree burns.

He wasn't going anywhere. Quickly, Angel took his weapons.

"Ayuda."

Help? The man was lucky Angel didn't slit his throat, and a few days ago he might have done just that. But not now. Now that he had Fiona. He'd still kill when necessary, but to take the life of a wounded, unarmed man would make him no better than Montoya.

"Callense," he said, holding up his knife and drawing a finger across his throat, showing the man what would happen if he interfered.

The man nodded and fell back against the ground.

Staying low, Angel continued on, looking for the rest of the soldiers and Montoya. Movement caught his eye and he recognized Montoya's tall, thin frame.

And beyond him, Fiona crouched against the building.

Montoya raised his weapon and held it to Fiona's head. Automatically, Angel raised his weapon, but as he fired off a round, someone grabbed his legs, knocking him sideways.

The soldier he'd let live had crawled the thirty feet to stop him. Rolling out of the way, Angel kicked the wounded man in the head, cursing the soldier's loyalty, and himself for letting him live, as he turned his attention back to Montoya.

The security chief had turned, and behind him, Fiona raised her gun. "Stop!" she shouted. "Everyone just stop!"

All action froze at her command. Slowly, Fiona pushed herself upward, keeping her gun on Montoya and her back pressed to the wall. Angel gave the soldier another kick in the head then rose.

Montoya turned and took a step toward her.

Fiona jammed her gun into his stomach, and Angel saw something on her face he'd never thought he'd see—blind hatred.

Other people might call it anger. Fear. He knew better. He'd seen that expression before. In his men. In the enemy. And in his mirror when he found out Isabel was dead. He'd been hurt, but the pain of a shattered heart was nothing compared to the overwhelming desire to kill the person who took her away.

And right now, Fiona wanted Montoya's death more than she wanted to breathe.

"Fiona!" Angel barked her name, desperate to stop her before she did something she couldn't take back.

She stopped, looking past Montoya's shoulder, her eyes wide with disbelief. "Angel?"

He hurried toward them, his gun on Montoya, catching more movement out of the corner of his eye. "Drop your weapons," Angel shouted in Spanish as he reached Montoya. "Or he dies."

The click of a weapon being cocked caught his attention. The security chief stiffened. Apparently, not everyone was as loyal as the soldier who tackled him. Damn it, Angel thought. Grabbing Montoya, he swung the man around, using him as a shield to cover both himself and Fiona.

"*Traidor,*" someone shouted. A shot rang out, followed by silence and the familiar thud of a body hitting the ground as one of Montoya's men shot another.

The rest hesitated, as if waiting for either Fiona or Angel to make a mistake. He had to work fast, before someone got cocky and took a shot at them. "*Tiren sus armas,*" he shouted again. "*¡Ahora!*"

The men in his field of vision hesitated, then placed their weapons on the ground, but he knew there were holdouts. "Tell the others to come forward and do as I say," Angel said in

Spanish. Montoya glanced back over his shoulder and Angel jammed his gun in deeper, making the man flinch. "Do it."

"Has lo que te dice, tiren sus armas," Montoya shouted. *"¡Ahora!"* Three more men appeared and all laid down their weapons.

It was a start, but far from what Angel considered a victory. He and Fiona were outnumbered. It wouldn't be long before the men rushed them. They had to bug out and fast.

"Señor, you seem as if you need some assistance."

Angel turned to see Don Marcos at his side. Behind him, the villagers secured the rest of the soldiers.

He'd forgotten the man and his people in his worry over keeping Fiona safe and dealing with Montoya and his men. "What do you have in mind?" he asked.

"Leave. Now. We will take their weapons. You take their vehicle."

"And them?" Fiona asked, her eyes glittering. "What will you do with them?"

"What would you like me to do with them, *señora?"* Don Marcos asked, pressing his M-16 into Montoya's chest.

Fiona hesitated, and Angel took her hand, calling her attention to himself. "Fiona." He squeezed her fingers. "Let me make this decision."

"Why?" she asked, her voice distant. "Why do you make the hard decisions? Why not me?"

He needed to keep her safe, both body and soul, but he couldn't tell her that. The words were too hard, even for a mercenary. "You asked me to do a job," he said. "And this is part of it."

"Life and death," she said. She stared at his hand then turned her attention to his face. Her eyes were more focused, and Angel almost sighed in relief.

"Yes."

The truck still burned, but she didn't flinch from looking at it. Instead, she cocked her head, and he knew she was trying to make sense of the scene.

With Montoya at gunpoint, Angel stood in front of her, blocking her view. "There's nothing there to see."

She peeked around him. "You killed them, didn't you?"

"Two men in the front. A few in the back," he said, watching her to see if she saw the monster beneath his skin. The man who killed and justified it.

"Them or us?" she asked.

"Yes." At the very least, maybe she understood they had to survive.

She took a deep breath and her blue eyes met his. "Thank you."

Chapter 11

"You will not succeed in this, *señorita,*" Montoya said.

His hands and ankles bound with zip ties taken from the other soldiers, Montoya sat on the ground in front of Fiona, back against the wall that surrounded Don Marcos's hacienda. Behind her, the villagers were picking up weapons as Angel stripped the remaining truck of anything that might be useful.

"You speak English," Fiona noted, modulating her voice to make sure he didn't hear the anger in her voice. Bullies like Montoya thrived on power. She'd give him nothing.

"Of course," Montoya said. "Did you think I was ignorant?"

"Not at all." She glanced down at him, pointing her M-16 at his head. Then his chest. His groin. His knee. Then back to his head.

His eyes never left her face. Her fingers tightened on the trigger. One squeeze and this would all be over. "I think you're a monster."

"Fiona." Angel walked past them, a box of grenades in his arms, the subtext in his voice telling her to stay cool.

"I'm not going to shoot him," Fiona said, flashing a smile in Montoya's direction. "I just have a few things I want to say."

"Are you using your words or your gun?"

She rolled her eyes. "Please don't talk to me as if I were a child."

Angel pulled her close. "Then stop being a bully."

"I'll use my words, okay?" Fiona jerked away, irritated that she had to justify her actions and emotions to anyone—even Angel.

"I'm not thrilled with your words, either," Angel said.

She glared at him.

He sighed. "But since you insist, keep it short. We're leaving in a few minutes."

She kept her victory smile hidden. It seemed she'd managed to teach him that sometimes she was going to do as she pleased, no matter what he said.

"A few minutes are all I'll need," she said.

Shaking his head, Angel walked away.

Fiona knelt down, her weapon trained on Montoya. "You took someone away from me." She kept her voice low, saving her words for herself and for the man at the other end of her gun. "You killed my friend."

Montoya never broke her gaze. "I cannot change that."

She hated him and the way he stared at her, as if his actions were those of a righteous man. He kept staring at her, and only the knowledge that she'd have to set her weapon down kept her from wiping off his expression with the back of her hand. "Why did you kill Maria and Tony?"

"For Colombia," Montoya replied. "Everything I do, I do for my country."

Fiona almost reeled in surprise. "Excuse me?"

"Colombia is besieged with kidnappings. Murders. Rebel whores like Maria contribute to the chaos instead of offering a solution," he said, his voice heated.

"Tony was no longer a member of RADEC."

"How was I to know that?" His gaze was as sincere as his voice, making Fiona bristle with indignation.

"You shot a woman in cold blood," she reminded him. "Acted as if she were free then gunned her down."

"I shot a terrorist," Montoya said. "I took no pleasure in her death, but she was a threat to my country and my people. Our way of life. RADEC is a threat. As a reporter, you should know that."

"RADEC wants to build a better world."

"Out of the ashes of what they would destroy," Montoya said.

"Then talk to them," she replied. She knew her plea meant little, but still she had to speak. "Work with them."

"They are ignorant rebels. There is no reasoning with the foolish."

God help her, she believed him. Not that what he did was either right or excusable but that he believed his actions were justified and that RADEC was a threat.

Montoya pressed her. "Give me the tape. Let me go. Help me save my people from the bloodshed that would come with a revolution."

A woman shrieked, and Fiona glanced behind her to see what was left of the men in the burned truck fall from the cab and into the dirt. Her eyes widened in horror.

"See, *señorita.*" Montoya's voice was tight. "Your man is no better than me. He kills to protect you. For what he thinks is right."

She couldn't argue with his logic. Damn, he was convincing.

Then she saw the familiar glint in his gaze. The same satisfaction she'd seen earlier when he thought he had her.

Her blood ran cold, making her shiver.

She pinched the bridge of her nose, stunned that she'd almost fallen for his pack of lies. He's good, she realized. Very good.

But no matter what he said, he didn't do this for Colombia and the greater good. He did this for himself and the power that would come with ruling a country and its people. "You're wrong," she said. "Angel does what he does when forced. He doesn't seek out death. You offered rewards for our capture. You chased us. You even accused us of the murders *you* committed."

Realizing he'd lost her, Montoya's mouth twisted into a sneer. "You are an ignorant bitch and should kill me now, because I will find you again and when I do, I will kill you."

She leaned in and raised the muzzle of the M-16. "Good advice."

His eyes widened, and a little thrill of satisfaction at breaking his cool raced through her. She could end this here. Now.

But would that make her a monster or a hero?

Before she resolved the inner conflict, a hand leaned down and gripped the barrel of her gun, pulling it upward. Angel stood over them.

"Time to go."

She frowned. So close. She stood, certain that if she didn't then Angel would pick her up and force her to go.

"Jeep," Angel said.

She walked over but after less than a dozen steps through the dirt, she realized Angel wasn't following. She turned on her heel to see him talking to Montoya.

What the hell was he saying?

Before she could go back, Angel rose and came toward her.

"What was that about?" she asked.

"Nothing much. Just that it would behoove him to return to Bogotá and leave us alone."

She raised a brow. "You said *behoove?*"

He chuckled. "Not exactly."

The sound of his laughter brought a smile to her mouth and by the time they reached the jeep, she felt better about leaving Montoya alive. As much as she loathed the man, she didn't want to become a female version of him—killing people then justifying her actions.

Don Marcos was waiting at the jeep, a basket in his hands. "Food and water," he said, setting it into the backseat.

She set her weapon beside it. "What about the other cars?"

"We will keep them," Don Marcos said. "We can always use trucks for hauling cargo."

"Emeralds?" she asked.

Don Marcos chuckled. "Pretty green stones, *señorita*. Just pretty green stones that some people seem to enjoy."

Fiona smiled. "Of course." And that was what she would say if anyone ever asked.

"And the men and Montoya?" Angel asked. "What about them?"

Don Marcos shrugged. "As much as I would like to end their lives, I cannot." He touched the gold cross that hung around his neck. "They will be sent home safe to their families. Late for dinner, perhaps, but they will arrive alive and unharmed."

Fiona sighed, disappointed despite her decision that it was best to rise above her baser, more murderous, desires. "I understand. This isn't your fight. It's mine."

"You are wrong, *chica*," Don Marcos said, "It is for Colombia. It is my fight."

Angel tapped her shoulder. "We need to leave. I want to make as much distance as possible before nightfall."

Fiona climbed into the jeep, thankful for the village's help and sorry that she'd brought Montoya to its doorstep.

"*Señor,* thank you for everything," Angel said, shaking Don Marcos's hand then starting the jeep.

"Take care of each other," Don Marcos said.

Fiona smiled, noticing how he applied the directive to them both instead of just Angel, as he had earlier. "We will," she said.

Angel started the jeep and turned up the hill, heading back the way they'd come. They didn't have much time before nightfall and needed to get as far away as possible. Fiona turned in the seat, watching as the village and its inhabitants shrank from sight. They crested the hill, and she turned, facing forward.

Angel patted her knee. "You okay?"

That was a loaded question. She'd called Montoya the monster but had found the capacity for evil in herself, as well. "Fine," she said.

The sound of a gunshot reverberated through the air.

Simultaneously, they looked to each other.

Angel stopped the jeep, kicking up a spray of dirt and rock. Rooting around in the back, he retrieved a set of binoculars and walked toward the ridge. Just before his silhouette crested the hill, he lay on his stomach, crawling the rest of the way with Fiona following in the same fashion. "Oh, hell," he said.

Fiona blood chilled. "What's going on?"

He handed them to her. She put them to her eyes, hands trembling at the thought of what she might see. Quickly, she adjusted the lenses. Her breath caught in her throat. Another truck of soldiers had arrived. The villagers held them off but Montoya and the others were being released.

"Where did they come from?" she whispered. "Where?"

"This is my fault," Angel said.

"How?" She stared at the scene below. Horrified but unable to turn away.

"I should have known there'd be more."

"How would you know that?"

"Montoya might be the bad guy, but that doesn't mean he's stupid. He's a trained warrior and a smart leader. There was backup, and I'd bet my last gun that Montoya missed a 'check in' call."

"And that brought in the rest of his team," Fiona finished.

There was more movement in the village. Don Marcos was talking to Montoya, his hands gesturing as he spoke.

Someone handed Montoya a gun.

"Run," she whispered, knowing it wouldn't matter. Montoya would kill Don Marcos despite his connections, and there was nothing she or Angel could do about it. "Turn away and run."

Montoya raised the weapon and another gunshot sounded.

Don Marcos fell to the ground. The villagers ran to their fallen benefactor. Anna's mouth opened in a cry of suffering. Montoya's men walked back to the remaining truck, seemingly undisturbed by what had happened.

Then Montoya looked up the hill. Though Fiona knew he couldn't see her, he seemed to stare into her.

Stunned, Fiona dropped the binoculars. "He's dead," she said, "Don Marcos is dead."

"Dammit." Angel tugged at Fiona's arm. "We have to go."

"What about the villagers? We should go help them."

"No can do," Angel said.

"Why?" Her pulse raced and her stomach churned at the thought of Montoya killing yet another person.

He shook his head. "He's armed and has more men. We've lost the element of surprise, and you're not wearing body armor." He glanced through the binoculars. "The rest of the villagers are fine. Montoya is leaving."

"Are you sure?"

"Yes." He started crawling backward, pulling her with him. "He's coming this way. We've got to leave. Now."

Numb with horror and guilt, Fiona let herself be guided.

Angel had said they'd be safe when they were out of Colombia and the tape was aired, but she was beginning to wonder if that were true. Despite her determination to do the right thing, people kept dying.

Sitting on an army blanket they'd found in the jeep and brought along, Fiona stared into the fire. Luckily, outrunning Montoya had been easy. His truck was overloaded and made for the road, not charging over rocky mountaintops.

Blowing up the bridge after crossing it didn't hurt. Since then, they'd driven in silence in the dark, each lost in their thoughts. They'd finally run out of gas and hiked for another hour, as far as they could in the darkness, before Angel decided the risk was too great. Tomorrow, they would walk the ridge and, with luck, get through one of the passes that went through the Cordillera Occidental mountain range and from there to safety.

Picking up a stick, Fiona poked at the fire.

"If we'd gone back, there's nothing we could have done except die," Angel said.

She knew he was right. Didn't doubt the logic of his words. But logic was little comfort when faced with guilt that refused to remain silent. "I know," she said. "We did what we needed to do."

Sitting down, Angel put his arm around her shoulder and pulled her close. "You did nothing wrong."

It was sweet that he wanted to absolve her of any wrongdoing, but it wasn't that easy. "It was just as much my responsibility. I brought Montoya to the village. He came because of me." She reached into her pocket and pulled out the tape. "And this."

Angel took the tape from her hands and set it aside, and kissed her hair. "It's not your fault."

He might believe that, but she didn't. Everything was her fault. If she hadn't come to Colombia, Tony would be alive. Don Marcos wouldn't have been shot down like an animal. Everyone would be safe.

But she had come, and now she wasn't sure how she was going to face herself or anyone else. "How do you deal with the guilt?" she whispered. "How do you get by?"

"I used to drink," Angel said.

Remembering when she first met him—tired of life and so distant that he might as well have been on another planet—Fiona leaned against Angel, thankful for his presence and change of perspective. "And now?"

He shrugged. "Fiona, don't make the mistake in thinking that I feel guilt about what happened."

Stunned, she sat up. "Someone died because of us."

"Someone died, yes," Angel said, his eyes black in the firelight. "But we didn't pull the trigger. Montoya did."

"Don Marcos died," Fiona insisted, willing Angel to empathize with her overwhelming emotions.

"He knew what he was getting into. When we came into that village, on foot and with you half dead, he knew. And he decided to help. To take action."

Fiona squeezed her hands into fists, beating the air. "You don't get it. You just don't get it. Someone is dead."

"No, *you* don't get it. You're belittling his sacrifice by making it all about you."

Familiar anger warmed her, and she glared at him. Angel grabbed her hand, his touch firm but gentle. She tried to jerk away but he held her in his grip, determined to make her understand. "I've seen death. I know death. Hell, we're best friends. I don't fear it and neither did Don Marcos. But he died a good death—protecting what mattered."

Fiona squeezed her eyes shut, willing herself to not cry. "He didn't even know me."

"He knew you wanted to save his people. To help his country. To stop Montoya from taking over. He was a wise man who'd seen a lot in his life and knew the score. Don't make the mistake of thinking otherwise."

Angel made sense. But that didn't stop the tears. He pulled her close again, and she cried against him. He kissed her hair again and whispered to her that it would be okay. That she was brave and kind and that he'd make sure the sacrifices weren't for nothing.

She didn't believe a word of it, but she wanted to. Needed to. She lifted her face to his and kissed him, willing herself to believe him.

"Make me forget," she whispered against his lips, desperate for solace. "Just for tonight, make me forget."

Angel cupped her head in his hands and crushed his mouth

against hers, breaking the kiss only long enough to yank her shirt off and toss it into the dark. "I'll do what I can."

She bit his ear, not satisfied with the response. "If you're tender, I'll kill you," she whispered.

"Have it your way." Angel almost growled the words. Leaning her backward, he took a nipple in his mouth, tugging on it hard enough to leave a bruise.

She didn't care. It was what she needed. Physical pain to blot out the feelings that seemed to overwhelm her soul. "Harder," she whispered.

Breathing hard and barely able to control himself, Angel rolled Fiona onto her back. He'd never wanted anyone like he wanted her. In the sane part of his brain he knew it might be an aftereffect of the day's events, but he didn't care.

He stroked Fiona's hair away from her cheek. She glowed, the flames illuminating her hair and skin.

Then again, perhaps it had nothing to do with adrenaline.

He'd never felt this way. Not even about Isabel. He'd loved her. Mourned her. Would never forget her and the future he'd lost the day she died. But theirs was a love built on tempers and chaos and opposite natures.

Fiona was different. She had Isabel's curiosity but she was steadier. He caressed her cheek, remembering how he'd accused her of wanting accolades more than the truth.

He couldn't have been more wrong.

She smiled up at him and wrapped her arms around his neck, pulling him to her. "Quit staring," she said, biting his neck.

He ran his hands down her sides then his thumbs around the inside of her waistband. Pushing up her skirt, he yanked her panties off, tossing them in the vicinity of her shirt.

Unzipping his pants, he pushed them off then hesitated. "We don't have protection," he said, wanting her more than he wanted water or air or a decent bed, but there were consequences to action.

"I'm clean," she whispered. "No STDs."

"Same here," he replied. "How about..." He flattened his hand on her stomach.

She rested her hand on top of his. "I have one of those once-a-month shots. I can't get pregnant."

The little ripple of disappointment caught him by surprise. They'd make a beautiful child, he realized. Her brains. His street smarts. Her blond hair. His olive skin. He moved his hand up her torso, and took a swatch of her hair in his fist.

He missed her pale curls. She wore the black well, but it was a shield to keep her safe.

"Are you going to make love to me or just stare?" Fiona asked, wrapping her legs around his hips and pulling him to her.

His erection pressed against her, and he groaned. Sitting up, he guided her until she straddled him, her legs gripping the outside of his thighs.

Slowly and wanting to enjoy every inch, he pulled her onto his length until she was wrapped around him in all ways that mattered. The position gave her the control, but he loved the torture. Wrapping his arms around her, he ran his hands down her back, caressing her skin.

She shuddered in response and rolled her hips. "You feel amazing," she whispered.

Her heat was exquisite but not enough. Hands on her waist, Angel pulled her upward then lowered her, barely able to maintain control.

"Again," Fiona whispered, adjusting her legs so she could rise as she pleased.

Angel wasn't sure if she was speaking to him or to herself, and he didn't care. All he knew was that the heaven that was Fiona was more than a mercenary like himself deserved, but he was going to revel in her presence.

Eyes closed, biting her lower lip, Fiona rode him, her pace

increasing with each stroke. Angel held her tighter, the heat of her skin growing warmer with each second.

His own breath was harsh in his ears and his body tightened. He wouldn't be able to hold out much longer.

"Harder," she whispered. "I need to feel it. Feel you."

With a groan, Angel flipped her onto her back. Pinning her hands above her head, he thrust into her. She cried out and he hesitated, thinking he'd hurt her.

"More." Fiona almost screamed the words, wrapping her legs around him.

He thrust again, and she shuddered around him, crying out as she climaxed.

This time, there was no control and he followed her, crying out even as he kissed her.

Chapter 12

Angel stopped at the side of the trail, turning back when he realized that Fiona was no longer behind him. Bent over with her hands on her knees, she looked as if she might faint.

That couldn't be good. He knew the rising altitude was hard on her, and it didn't help that neither of them had slept last night. He walked back to her. "You okay?"

Her pale skin was bright red and she'd sweated through her T-shirt. As much as he liked looking at her legs, she needed clothing that offered her more protection from the brush and branches. She nodded. "It's not the heat—"

"—it's the humidity?" he finished.

She shrugged. "Sorry for the cliché. I'm too tired for original sarcasm."

Straightening, she put her hands on her hips and leaned back, stretching. "It's like trying to breathe through a wet washcloth, for pity's sake." She flashed him a sideways glance. "You seem fine. Sweaty, but fine. What's with that?"

"Going to the gym is no substitute for spending a lifetime as a soldier," Angel said.

"I guess not."

"How are your feet?" She wore a pair of sandals Don Marcos had provided. Built to last, they were more serviceable than the skirt, but still didn't provide her the protection he'd like.

"Good," she said. "Just tired."

He hoped that was true. They still had a few days of walking ahead of them. While the mountain range was scalable in this area of Colombia, that didn't mean it was an easy hike.

A twig snapped behind them, and instantly Angel straightened.

Were they being followed? He unslung the M-16 from his shoulder.

"What's wrong," Fiona whispered, taking hers in hand, as well.

Angel put a finger to his lips. He didn't think it was Montoya's men on their trail. His team didn't have the grace and skill needed to follow undetected. Perhaps an animal. Or one of the indigenous tribes that Don Marcos had mentioned.

He hoped for an animal.

Otherwise, it meant he was slipping.

He motioned Fiona to come closer. "We might have picked up a tail. Stay close." Putting his weapon away but ready to arm himself in seconds, he continued the hike, waiting to see if their tail would make himself—or herself—known.

But for another sweaty, muscle-aching mile, the only sounds were birdcalls and the occasional monkey screech.

They reached an open part of the ridge, and he stopped, handing Fiona a canteen. "What do you think it was?" she asked, handing the canteen back.

"Animal. Overactive imagination. Paranoia."

Fiona chuckled. "I pick number three."

Angel grinned then took a swig of water. It was warm but did the job. "It's an option."

Her laughter faded. "But you don't think we're being followed? Right?"

Angel sighed, eager for their journey to end so she'd never have to ask questions like that again.

She deserved laughter. Not dodging bullets, running for her life or tromping through the mountains with next to no supplies. "I don't think so." He nodded toward the dense growth that surrounded them. "The jungle would be a helluva lot quieter if someone were in there waiting. Animals don't like predators in their midsts and that's what humans are—predators."

"Don't I know it," Fiona muttered.

Another twig snapped and the hairs on the back of Angel's neck rose. In seconds, he freed his weapon, pointing the muzzle toward the sound.

"I thought you said there was no one there?" Fiona whispered. There was no terror in her voice. Just resignation in light of another crappy situation.

"I'm still not sure there is," Angel said.

Fiona opened her mouth to speak and he raised a hand, asking for silence. She nodded. Waited.

"Who's there?" Angel called out.

Thirty seconds later, there was a rustling in the bushes and two men rose from the jungle scrub. Seemingly unarmed, they were both considerably shorter than either Fiona or Angel, with black hair that reached their shoulders.

Dressed in unadorned, rough clothing, they didn't carry weapons, unless one considered a walking stick a weapon.

Indigenous, but were they the friendlies or the hostiles? He stepped in front of Fiona, shielding her.

"*Hola,*" Angel said. "*¿Habla español?*"

Both shook their heads, suspicion in the hard gazes.

"This should be fun," Fiona said. "What do we do now?"

"Depends on what they want," Angel said.

"If they want us dead?"

"Then we make the first move."

Slowly, the men moved forward. Angel leveled his M-16 at them. "Stop right there," he said. They froze, but sneered at the weapons with obvious disgust.

That was a good sign, Angel thought. They recognized a gun. That made them less likely to be stupid.

The one on the right whispered to the one on the left. He nodded then called out in a language Angel didn't recognize. It sounded more like a serious of birdcalls than anything human.

"What the hell?" Fiona whispered. "What was that?"

Once again, the hairs on the back of Angel's neck rose, and he knew he'd seriously underestimated these people, whoever they were. In seconds, he and Fiona were surrounded by twenty men.

"I hope they're not cannibals," Fiona said, keeping her voice low.

Once they were surrounded, he'd told her to give up her weapon, since there was no way they were going to defeat twenty men. Not without himself or Fiona being hurt or killed. So, Fiona had handed over her gun, and he'd allowed their captors to escort them to the village on the other side of the ridge.

Primitive but sturdy grass huts with conical tops circled a patch of land scraped bare of jungle. Now, they sat inside one of the huts, waiting for fate to toss them a new hand.

"You watch too many movies," Angel said. He wasn't worried about being boiled for a snack. He was worried about being killed for trespassing on the locals' land. Most indigenous peoples avoided outsiders, but that didn't mean they wouldn't, or couldn't, protect themselves.

The question was, what did protection mean to them? A knife in the neck, or an escort out of their territory at some point?

He prayed their captors didn't know about the bounty on their heads. They might shun the modern world, but money spoke louder than tradition.

"So what do we do?" Fiona asked.

"Other than wishing I had a weapon, we play nice."

"Easy enough," Fiona said.

The wooden door to the hut opened. Both Angel and Fiona leapt to their feet. A woman so petite she might have been a child motioned them to come out.

Angel nodded to the woman then to Fiona. "Let's do this. Nice and easy."

Slowly, keeping his hands out to the sides and trying to appear as nonthreatening as possible despite the fact that he towered over everyone in the village, Angel followed the woman. Fiona stayed close behind him.

A crowd had gathered. Men. Women. Even the children. It seemed as if the entire village of perhaps fifty people was waiting for them.

"I feel like Gulliver," Fiona said. "What do we do?"

"Say hi," Angel suggested. "And smile."

"That's just great," Fiona whispered. "Smile. That's the plan."

"You're the girl. You look friendlier," Angel replied. "Just do it."

Slowly, Fiona raised her hand and waved. *"Hola."*

No one moved. Or smiled. Or waved back.

"That went well," Fiona said, her tone tinged with sarcasm. "Do you think this is one of the friendly tribes? We should have asked Don Marcos for more information."

A murmur went through the crowd at Fiona's mention of Don Marcos, and Angel heard someone say *El Sabio.*

The Wise One.

Perhaps that was Don Marcos?

A petite old man in a simple white skullcap broke through the small group and came forward. Though elderly, he had an aura of power about him. Either a shaman or their chief.

Or *El Sabio,* though he couldn't imagine giving a Spanish name to one of their own.

The elderly man stopped in front of Angel, craning his neck upward. He pointed to himself. "Eizo."

"Eizo." Angel repeated his name then pointed to himself and Fiona, saying their names in return.

Eizo's dark eyes twinkled with youth despite the wrinkles that lined his face. He stared into Angel's eyes.

The old man's gaze was disturbing, like looking into the night sky—one could see forever and it gave Angel a sense of eternity—and he had to force himself to return the stare.

Around him, the world slowed then stilled. Soon, there was nothing but the beat of his heart and the blackness of Eizo's gaze.

Finally, the old man turned away, but not before Angel caught a glimpse of the smile on his lips. Angel breathed a sigh of relief.

"What was that about?" Fiona asked.

"What do you mean?" Angel asked.

But before she answered, the old man was in front of her, whispering. She shifted from one foot to another then stilled as Eizo held her gaze.

A minute passed. Three. Then five. Had he done the same thing? Angel wondered. Stared into the old man's eyes, caught like a mouse in a trap?

This was getting weird, he decided. Almost too weird. He wondered if he should stop it.

Then suddenly, the old man blinked and began chattering to the rest of the villagers.

"You okay?" Angel asked, putting his arm around Fiona. She looked up at him. Her eyes were clear. Bright. He wanted to ask her what she'd seen but somehow that seemed akin to asking someone about a confession to a priest.

"How long was I under?" she asked.

"Five minutes, give or take." Before he had time to ask the same question, the crowd of people parted before them. Eizo motioned for them to follow, but Angel hesitated. It wouldn't be the first time he was treated as a guest only to end up fighting for his life.

"Vamos. Vamos," Eizo said in an accent that was almost impossible to understand.

Someone pushed Angel forward. It seemed they didn't have a choice. Taking Fiona's hand, he followed the elder.

Eizo led them through the village to a hut on the outskirts. Twice as small as the rest, it was unimpressive. They entered. There were no windows but a fire was lit in the middle of the room, keeping it from utter darkness. There was no furniture. Not even a blanket to sit on.

Eizo sat on one side of the pit and pointed to the opposite side.

"What the hell is going on," Fiona said in a stage whisper. "This is starting to freak me out."

"Do as he says," Angel said. "This might be freaky, but so far they're harmless, and I'd like to keep it that way."

Eizo asked, *"¿Don Marcos, esta bien?"*

Was he well?

"¿Esta bien?" Eizo pressed.

So Don Marcos was El Sabio. Apparently the old man had been a helluva lot more than he'd let on.

"What are you going to tell him?" Fiona asked.

"Not the truth," Angel replied. The last thing he wanted to do was piss these people off. *"Sí, Don Marcos esta bien."*

Eizo smiled. Opening up a small bag at his side, he tossed a handful of leaves onto the fire. A cloud of smoke filled the air. Cautiously, Angel sniffed. Whatever the shaman burned smelled sweet.

Eizo tossed on more leaves and the smoke increased until it filled the hut.

In front of Angel, the fire danced and swayed. Sang like a choir of angels. Eizo grew as tall as the room and suspiciously younger.

They'd been drugged. Angel's heart raced as panic tried to grab him. He pushed the sensation aside. He had to get Fiona out of the hut.

"Fiona?" His voice boomed in his ears as loud as a gunshot. She didn't answer. The air seemed as thick as syrup as he turned to her. Slowly, he poked her in the arm. Slumped over with her hair covering her face, she didn't respond.

"Oh, hell," he muttered, and then there was nothing but the fire.

Fiona inhaled the smoke, trying not to choke on the sweet scent. It reminded her of a Temazcal she'd had in Mexico. The healing, cleansing ritual began when one stripped naked and entered a natural lodge heated with stones and scented with healing herbs. It ended with a full-body massage.

As interesting as the villagers seemed, she hoped she didn't end up naked.

The smoke grew thicker, and she closed her eyes. The ground beneath her swayed. Outside of herself, a chanting began and she wished she knew what Eizo said.

"Does it matter?" a familiar voice asked.

She opened her eyes. Sitting next to her was Tony. Same hair. Same dark eyes. Same crappy camera sitting on the ground next to him.

But Tony was dead. Whoever this was in front of her was a ghost. Or she'd finally lost her mind. Possibly both.

He grinned. "Miss me?"

It sounded like Tony, and whoever, *whatever,* he was, smiled at her with that familiar, crooked grin.

"Tony?" Hands shaking, she reached for him. He took her hand in his. He was solid to her touch. Alive and real and not dead. She yanked him close, eyes tearing even as she wanted to smack him for letting her think he'd died. "Oh, my God, what are you doing here? I thought you were—"

He put up a hand. "Don't say it, Fiona. Don't say it or you'll make it true."

"What do you mean, I'll make it true?"

He patted her hand. "Fiona, think about it. You know this isn't real."

But she wanted it to be.

"Wanting it to be doesn't make it so," Tony said. "You know that."

She did, but that didn't mean she had to like it. "So what's the point?" she said. "What's going on?"

"Always down to business," Tony said.

Fiona shrugged, not sure how to respond to a hallucination.

Tony sighed. "I have a question of my own."

"What?"

"What are you doing?"

"What do you mean?"

"This running around with a gun. With Angel."

"You sent me to him," Fiona protested. "And why should I have to justify myself to a drug-induced figment of my imagination?"

"You don't," Tony countered. "Angel is very good at what he does, but I didn't send you to him so you could become him. His job is to protect you. To make sure you do your job."

"Which is what? Report?" In light of everything that had happened, her job seemed insignificant.

"You do more than that. You know it. I know it. You tell the truth. It's your gift."

Fiona scrubbed her face with her hands. "I've seen what

happens here. Good people die. Bad people walk away. I'm not sure the truth will change that. Not here. Not anymore."

Tony sighed. "It's what you do. It's what you are. You hold a mirror up to the world and force it to *see*."

She turned away. "I don't do that. Not anymore."

"Do you really believe that?" he asked, daring her with his eyes.

She wanted to say yes. It would be so much easier. But she couldn't call Tony a liar. When she was younger, she'd seen injustice and done nothing. They were small injustices—a cruel comment here or a lie there. But even a small lie could change a life in an unexpected way.

Now, she wasn't that person. Especially not when it was Tony questioning her. She leaned into her hands. "No."

"I didn't think so." There was a scuffling noise and when she raised her head, Tony stood over her. "I know you're tough. You watched me die. You saw a man shot in the leg. And you dyed your hair that truly awful color."

She raised a brow. "Gee, thanks. Nice of you to notice."

"Sorry, but I call 'em as I see 'em." He didn't sound the least bit apologetic. "And you are tough, I'm not going to deny that you're strong, but now you have to do one more thing. Something even harder than pulling the trigger."

"What?" she asked, though she suspected she already knew the answer.

"Be the reporter I know you are. Tell my story and bring Montoya to justice." He smiled down at her. "Besides, you're a crappy shot."

She chuckled even as her eyes welled with tears again. "Yeah, let's see how *you* do in a dress."

"Maybe in the next life," he said.

She blinked back tears then Tony was gone. If he was ever there, she thought as she realized she was sitting in front of the fire with Angel and Eizo.

She rubbed her eyes. They were dry. No tears. No Tony. Not really.

As real as the hallucination was, it was still just a hallucination. Tony was dead, and he wasn't coming back to offer quips and sage advice.

But he'd done just that, she realized. Or her subconscious had. Either way, the point was made that she had to tell Tony's story. Show the world that Montoya was a monster who took life for no reason—no matter what he claimed.

That was what she did, she reminded herself. When she first met Angel, she told him that she told stories that mattered. It was still true. The truth was still in her, and she was determined to share it with the world.

Eizo smiled at her. *"¿Bueno?"*

She nodded. She'd found herself again. Her purpose. *"Bueno,"* she replied with a smile.

Chapter 13

"Donkeys?" Fiona asked, casting the animals a wary glance.

Their guns had been returned to them, and Angel was checking them out but took a moment to follow Fiona's gaze. Two burros were being fitted with halters. "They're burros."

Fiona raised a dark brow and wariness turned to mild disgust. "You say burro, I say an animal with large, bitey teeth," she countered. "I'm not riding it. I'll walk, thank you."

Angel chuckled. She dodged bullets, braved rapids, but drew the line at riding a beast of burden? He'd have never thought that animals were her sticking point.

"It's just a burro," he said. "They're probably safe."

"Angel!" He turned at hearing his name. Eizo walked toward them carrying a cloth satchel. He pressed it into Angel's hands. Angel peeked inside. It held their canteen, fruit and what might be dried meat of some kind.

Taking out the canteen, Angel tried to hand the rest back. "Too much," he said. These people were barely scraping by; the last thing he wanted to do was take their food.

Eizo shook his head no and turned to leave, but not before Angel saw the disappointment in his eyes.

Hell, he'd insulted the old man. "Eizo!"

The other man turned around. Angel held up the bag and smiled. *"Gracias."*

Eizo's mouth broke into a wide, semitoothless smile.

"What is it?" Fiona asked, standing at his side.

"Food. Water."

"They're good people," she said.

"I can't argue that," Angel said. She smiled at him, seeming more relaxed since last night's drug-induced visions. No, he corrected himself. More at peace. More sure. And surprisingly, more determined, though there wasn't any reason for him to assume it.

Still, he had a feeling…

He wondered what she'd seen, but somehow, asking her would seem almost sacrilegious.

Besides, if he asked her about her vision she might ask about his in return, and he had no desire to describe his experience. Hell, he was still trying to figure out the disjointed images that were rife with flames, death, Isabel and Montoya.

The only thing he knew for certain was he had a purpose. To make sure Fiona lived. But he'd known that even before the vision.

"You okay?" Fiona asked. "You look uneasy."

Angel put his arm around her and pulled her close. "Just thinking."

"About?"

"That perhaps, when this is over, we'll find an interpreter and come back. Tell Eizo what truly happened to Don Marcos."

Fiona smiled. "So you think we'll make it out of this alive?"

"We will," he said, planting a brief kiss on her mouth.

She smiled against his mouth. "I think so, too."

God, he loved her optimism. Her belief in him. He ran a hand through her dark hair. "So, next step. Get to Buenaventura and *Last Ditch Effort.* Then out of Colombia."

Fiona gave the burro an uneasy glance. "And we'll do that how?"

The unexpected noise of an engine cut through the morning air, and a few seconds later, Eizo puttered between two huts on the back of a three-wheeler towing a wooden, two-wheeled trailer carrying sacks of what Angel thought might be grain.

Eizo got down and two of the villagers placed the sacks on the backs of the burros. Eizo beckoned Fiona to sit.

"My guess is that you will not have to brave the rabid burros."

She stuck out her tongue at him and climbed into the trailer.

Angel sat next to her, the wood creaking beneath his weight. The villagers crowded around them, smiling and waving as their driver, one of the young men of the village, shifted gears and pulled out of the little community, following a path just wide enough to accommodate the vehicle.

Eizo stood in front, and all the villagers continued to wave until the three-wheeler rounded a bend and they disappeared from sight.

"I'll miss them," Fiona sighed, leaning against Angel.

"Me, too." He wanted to stay with Eizo and his people. The village was secluded and that made it far safer than where they were headed.

He blinked, and in that instant, a vision from last evening's drug-induced hallucination flashed across his lids.

Isabel.

He froze, caught in the moment. Isabel didn't say a word. She didn't have to. She was a reminder that nothing and nowhere was safe, no matter how much he might want life to be otherwise.

She faded, and he opened his eyes, remembering with crystal clarity that there was a job to do if he wanted Fiona to live. To be safe. *Forever.*

Montoya had to die.

* * *

Fiona lay on her back, legs dangling over the edge of the cart, and watched the trees and sky pass as they made their way to the city. The smell of exhaust mixed with the rich scents of the jungle, and she wrinkled her nose.

Bored, she raised her left hand, flattening it against the sky. She liked the ring, and somehow, it didn't matter that it was meant for another. *Isabel.*

Angel had loved her enough to want to marry her. That meant she must have been special. Wonderful.

The thought that he might see her like that, *one day,* tickled the back of her mind. Fiona shut it down. Now was neither the time nor circumstance to entertain those thoughts.

Angel snorted in his sleep and turned over.

He could sleep anywhere, she mused, dropping her hand back to her side.

There was a thump and a shudder and the cart came to a sudden stop. In less time than it took her to wonder why they'd come to a halt, Angel went from dead sleep to wide awake. He sat up, M-16 in hand, taking stock of the area. "Stay down," he said, pressing on her stomach to keep her from rising.

She did as he asked, knowing that if they were in danger, now wasn't the time to argue. She'd learned that much.

In seconds, the M-16 was lowered. "It's clear."

Fiona sat up. "Where are we?"

He pointed down the path, and Fiona turned. Their driver had stopped at the edge of the jungle. Beyond them, perhaps a two miles away but visible, was a large city and just beyond that, the ocean.

"Welcome to Buenaventure," Angel said, jumping off the cart and stretching.

Goose bumps covered Fiona's arms, and she rubbed them with her hands. "Good," she said, her instincts screaming for her to turn around and run.

He glanced at her. "It is. We'll be at my boat by midnight and then we're out of here."

"And Montoya?"

Angel raked his hands through his hair in a gesture she now recognized as frustration. "I'd like to say that he won't know we're here, but he's not that dumb. We'll head into the city, keep a low profile and find a hideout until dark. Then we go for it."

"Why not stay here?"

"Gangs," Angel said.

"Good point."

He continued, "The last place we want to be is outside the city limits at night. Keep your head down and it'll be fine."

The goose bumps didn't disappear but Fiona nodded. She trusted Angel and his judgment. After a quick goodbye to their guide, they headed toward the city. The outskirts were much like Bogotá—crowded with hovels, trash in the streets, and people who didn't look anyone in the eye.

She wrinkled her nose at the combination of rotting trash, fish and smog. "What a pit," she muttered.

"We won't be here long," Angel said.

Two men walked toward them, but stopped chatting when they passed the couple. Fiona stiffened, waiting for the inevitable shout of *Gotcha!*

"Stay calm," Angel whispered. "They think you're pretty, nothing more."

"Great." Fiona watched the ground, counting cracks in the broken sidewalk while she hid her face as best she could. "Any thoughts on where we should hide?"

"There's a bar, Rubíes, a few blocks away."

"It's always a bar, isn't it?" Fiona asked, trying not to smile.

"Seems that way," he said, the tension in his voice belying his words. "I have friends there who can help us."

"Friends?" Fiona asked. She leaned in as they walked. "Mercenaries?"

Angel glanced over at her. "No. A rebel leader runs the place."

Even though Angel wasn't a member of RADEC, it didn't surprise Fiona that he knew more of its members. "How does one go from bar owner to rebel leader?" she asked, curious.

"It's the other way around. Xavier was a rebel leader first. The bar belonged to his brother, Roberto. When he was murdered—"

"By Montoya?" Fiona interrupted.

"Not directly, but yes, Montoya's men were responsible," Angel confirmed. "Anyway, Xavier took over the business. He keeps the bar as cover." He sped up his pace, signaling an end to the discussion, and Fiona went back to counting cracks.

She'd counted one hundred fifty cracks when Angel took her elbow and turned into an open doorway. She breathed a sigh of relief as the wooden door closed behind them.

This bar wasn't unlike the bar where she'd first met Angel. Dark. Only a few customers. And a single bartender. A few inches shorter than Angel, he was built the same with broad shoulders and muscular arms. But his hair was darker, pitch black. And longer.

Women would kill for that hair, she thought.

He glanced up as the door closed and his eyes widened. He left his towel on the bar and came around. *"¡Angel! ¡Ese!"*

Angel gripped the man's hand. *"Xavier. ¿Cómo estás?"*

"Bien. Bien." Xavier kissed Angel on both cheeks then grinned at Fiona—his teeth brilliant against his dark skin—and then turned back to Angel. "Who is your friend?" he asked, wiggling his eyebrows.

Great. Somehow, he'd managed to make asking who she was sound dirty. She raised a dark brow. "Fiona," she said and stuck out her hand.

Xavier kissed her knuckles. "You are very beautiful, *señorita.*"

His attention drifted to her left hand. "Or should I say *señora?*" He grinned at Angel. "Do I get to kiss the bride?"

"I don't think so," Angel said, pulling Fiona to his side with a smile. "Ignore him," he said to her. "He thinks he's charming."

"*Thinks* being the operative word," Fiona said, smiling.

Xavier held his hand over his heart. "I am wounded!" He pulled out a chair and offered it to Fiona. "Please," he said. "Let me buy you wine and convince you to leave this man. He is no good for you."

Fiona laughed and sat. "Do you have red?"

"For you, I will find some and if not, I will press the grapes myself."

He kissed her hand again before disappearing into a small room in the back of the bar.

"He's sweet," Fiona said as Angel took the seat across from her.

"He can be," Angel said. "But don't let that fool you. He's seen action."

"I figured as much or you wouldn't have brought me here." She reached over and took Angel's hand in hers. "How do you think he knew I spoke English?"

Angel's eyes narrowed. "Good question."

The door in the back opened and Xavier returned with three glasses on a tray. Walking carefully so as not to spill them, he sat back down. "Please," he said, offering them each a glass of ruby-red wine.

Fiona took a small sip and sighed in almost-ecstasy as the sweet liquid touched her throat. "Excellent, thank you."

"My pleasure," Xavier said. "As I said, I want to woo you away from this man before it is too late."

Angel rolled his glass between his hands. "Xavier, Fiona asked an interesting question."

Xavier grinned. "If I was available?"

"No." He set the glass down. "How did you know she spoke English?"

"All Americans speak English, no?" Xavier said, toasting Fiona.

A chill ran up Fiona's spine, and in that instant, Angel pulled his weapon. "I never said she was American."

Xavier set his glass down. "I was hoping this would be less distasteful." He nodded toward Angel's wine. "Drink."

Fiona's heart pounded in her ears and bile rose in her throat. She dropped her glass and it shattered on the floor. "You're trying to poison us."

Xavier frowned. "Of course not. We have questions first, but you will need more wine since you so carelessly spilled yours."

Thank God she hadn't drunk enough to knock her out. Not that it mattered. From what Xavier had said, they planned to kill her and Angel. Just. Not. Yet.

Her stomach flipped again. "Angel?"

He didn't look at her. Instead, he glared at Xavier. "Judas," he hissed, sweeping his glass off the table. In seconds two armed men emerged from the back room.

Xavier leapt to his feet and the men halted. "Me? You."

"How so?" Angel asked, grinding the words out.

"You killed Maria," he said. "And for what? A *gringa?*" He looked at Fiona, and this time there was no charm in his eyes. Just disgust and a fury so hot she thought it might burn her to ashes.

As much as he wanted to shoot his way out of the situation, Angel kept tight rein on his emotions. He and Fiona might make it out alive, but there was no room in his world for *might*.

He had to be sure.

"What makes you think we killed Maria?" Angel asked.

"It is everywhere," Xavier answered. "And we have a witness."

"Who? Montoya?" Fiona chimed in, her blue eyes narrowed in anger.

"No. One of our men."

Fiona's face paled. "Then your man is a traitor."

Xavier's jaw stiffened, and he gave a nod.

Reaction before thought. Angel reached, jammed an elbow into the man next to him, grabbing his weapon before he hit the ground and aiming it at Xavier.

He didn't hear the guns being cocked but the hairs on Angel's neck rose and he knew their muzzles aimed at his back.

"Angel…" Fiona said.

She didn't finish. She didn't need to. He heard the fear.

And she was right. If it were just him in this situation, he'd go for the gunfight. But with Fiona present, bullets weren't an option. Uncocking the weapon, he let it dangle from his fingertips.

Someone from behind grabbed it.

"You are a fool," Xavier said.

"Perhaps," Angel said. "But you know me. You know I would never kill Maria."

"You are a mercenary," Xavier said. "I do not know what you would do for money."

"Talk to Juan," Fiona said. "He was there when I first met Angel. He can vouch for Angel, even if he can't vouch for me."

Xavier kept his attention on Angel. "Who's Juan?"

Fiona frowned. "I thought he was part of the resistance."

"He is," Angel assured her.

"Perhaps," Xavier replied. "It's not as if we all know each other." He held out his hand, palm up. "Weapons."

Fiona put hers on the table, and one of the other men picked it up.

"All of them," Xavier said. Angel pulled the knife from his belt.

"Sorry, I don't have anything else," Fiona said.

"Revísenla," Xavier said, and one of the men pulled Fiona to her feet then slowly frisked her, enjoying it more than he should have.

Fury roared through Angel, and he took a step forward. Another man used a rifle to block his progress.

"Angel. It's fine," Fiona said.

"Listen to her, *ese*," Xavier said. Angel stopped, promising himself that one day the man would pay.

Fiona frowned at the man who kneeled at her feet but remained silent. Much to her credit, she didn't struggle, and in fact acted as if she didn't give a damn at all.

Good girl, Angel thought. Don't give them anything.

The man pulled out the tape from the pocket in her skirt. She stiffened, and he wondered if she would say or do anything. She didn't. The rebel handed the tape to Xavier. "*Nada*. She is clean," he said then pushed her back into her chair.

Her eyes never left the tape in Xavier's hand. "You're making a mistake," she said.

"Possibly." Xavier held the tape up. "What is on this?"

Angel hesitated. It would clear their names, but there was also the real possibility Xavier and his people would keep it as insurance. Plus, he wasn't even sure it was watchable since its soak in the river.

Fiona answered for him. "It's the last thing my cameraman taped. Maria Salvador's death."

Xavier's hand trembled and he stared at the tape as if it were the Holy Grail. "*If* what you say is true, we can use this to stop Montoya."

"That was the intention," Fiona said. "Help us."

"I must see this," Xavier said.

"You can't," Angel said. "It got wet. If you play it, you might destroy it, and then Montoya will get away with murder."

Xavier froze. "Convenient, isn't it?" He pocketed the tape, and what little sympathy they'd garnered exited from his eyes. "Liars."

"No!" Fiona said, trying to rise. Xavier pushed her back into the chair.

"Please, believe me," she pleaded, frustrated with the RADEC leader's stubbornness. "I want to help you and your people."

Xavier ran a hand over her dark hair. "Perhaps. Or perhaps not. Either way, this is no longer yours. It is ours."

"You can't take it," Angel said, willing himself not to tackle the man and take the tape. "Fiona has the resources to expose Montoya and his corruption to the world."

"The world?" Xavier sneered. "The world knows what Montoya is and the world doesn't care.

"If you are telling the truth and this tape is what you say it is, President Ramirez will have to listen to us. We can make our own terms."

"Unless Montoya is already too powerful," Angel countered. Xavier had to see that exposure was a better long-term goal than blackmail, and a helluva lot less risky for the members of RADEC. "Then he will kill you all and discredit the tape."

He took a step toward Xavier. "Fiona is a reporter. A reputable reporter. Let her tell your story."

"Trust me," Fiona pleaded. "Please."

Xavier shook his head, and Angel knew trust was the last thing the rebel leader would give. Not that he blamed him. Not really. Enemies were difficult to discern in Colombia. Friends even harder. "You're making a mistake," Angel said, his voice low.

Before Xavier could respond, the front door opened, and all heads turned.

"Duck!" Angel shouted, setting himself into motion even as he shouted to Fiona. Snapping his hand out, he grabbed Xavier's gun and slammed it into the wall. The gun went off, and the bullet bit into the floor.

Xavier's free hand came around in a jab and connected with the side of Angel's head. For a beat, Angel saw stars, but training won out over pain and he twisted the gun from Xavier's grasp as the rebel leader landed another punch.

Angel put the muzzle to Xavier's head, and then Xavier's fist halted midswing. His dark eyes bit into Angel's but he didn't say a word.

There was a scuffling behind him. "Fiona?" Angel said. "Are you okay?"

She appeared at his side. "Here," she said.

Damn, but she was learning quickly. "Get the tape." Carefully, she reached into Xavier's pocket, pulled out the tape and tucked it inside her blouse.

They had to act fast before the other men rallied.

"You, away from the door." The surprised old man who had acted as his unintentional distraction shuffled toward the bar. Keeping his weapon pointed at Xavier and Fiona behind him, Angel backed toward the door.

"We will find you," Xavier said. "And if not us, Montoya's men are everywhere."

"Thanks for the heads-up," Angel said. "What about Montoya? Is he here?" He knew Xavier and RADEC would keep track of Montoya's movements.

Xavier glared at him.

Angel pushed the muzzle of the gun into his friend's side. "Where is he?"

"There is a house next door to the State Building. He is there."

"Thanks."

"*De nada.* Really."

The other men stepped forward, guns still at the ready. *Morons.* "Drop them. Now. Or so help me, I will kill him," Angel said.

And he would. As much as he hated the thought of killing a friend, it was Fiona's life on the line and nothing, not even friendship, would make him put her in further danger.

"Get the door," he said over his shoulder.

Behind him, the door creaked open and sunlight shone in through the opening. "We're clear," Fiona said. "No cops."

"Don't follow us, Xavier," Angel said. "I'd hate to kill you or any of your men." Gun still pointed at the rebels, he and Fiona slid out the door and onto the street.

Chapter 14

"We've got to lose them," Angel muttered. They'd been tracked by Xavier's men since escaping the bar over an hour ago, and with the sun setting, their opponents would grow braver.

Angel led them south to an area that he could swear had been industrial just over a year ago. It was now a trendy tourist area. Warehouses still lined the streets, but now they housed restaurants, clubs and a few storefronts complete with mannequins.

Too many people for his taste, but a perfect place to shake a tail.

"We're being followed?" Fiona asked, glancing over her shoulder. "I didn't spot anyone. At least not lately."

Angel didn't bother to scan his surroundings. He didn't need to. "They're there. Trust me."

They reached a large complex of buildings that seemed to be the center for most of the partying. "Perfect," Angel said. "Crowds and lots of exits." Out of the corner of his eye, he spotted a familiar face. He couldn't remember the name but he definitely remembered the man's ability to kill.

If the rebels were that blatant, time was shorter than he thought. Taking Fiona's hand, he headed toward the largest warehouse. People swirled around them, and he pulled her close and tightened his grip. The last thing he wanted was to lose her in the crowds.

They walked faster, and the sound of salsa music caught his attention. One of the larger warehouses had been converted into a multiplex of sorts, and on the lower floor, flanked by a restaurant on either side, was a dance club—*La Máquina de la Danza,* according to the large neon sign.

He stopped midstep to assess the situation. The oversize door to the club was guarded by an equally oversize bouncer. And on a placard, written in hot-pink marker, was something about free salsa lessons prior to the night's partying.

He smiled. Not a perfect retreat, but the lights and sound would confuse anyone. And since it was part of the larger complex, there were staff hallways that connected the stores and doors that led out back.

"Come on," he said to Fiona, pulling her toward the club.

A small group of people approached the door—two men in suits and two women in dresses that left little to the imagination. The bouncer glanced at them, deemed them appropriate, and opened the door.

Another group dressed in casual, street clothes followed on the heels of the fancier group and moved to enter, but the bouncer put out a large, meaty hand, stopping them. There was a bit of a scuffle as one of the men argued with the large man and tried to push past.

It ended with the smaller man on the ground.

"We're not exactly dressed for a club," Angel said, watching the altercation. "That could be a problem."

"Or not," Fiona grinned. "Just let me work my mojo." Putting her back to the doorman, she unbuttoned her blouse almost to her waist and rolled the waistband of her skirt until her hem was hiked to midthigh. "I'll distract. You'll sneak in."

"I don't think so," Angel said, reaching over to rebutton her blouse. He could take a lot of things, but Fiona practically selling herself to save his ass was not one of them.

Fiona slapped his hand. "It's not like I'm going to sleep with the man. I just want him to think he has a shot."

"This is a bad idea," Angel said, unconvinced. "It'll attract attention."

"No," Fiona said. "This will." Raising her hand, she slapped Angel across the face. *"¡Cabrón!"*

Angel stared at her, surprised. "What the hell?"

"Go with it," she whispered. "We have to make the bouncer believe it."

"Believe what?" Angel asked, rubbing his cheek. "That you're insane? I think everyone thinks that." He noticed the tail he'd spotted a few minutes ago grinning.

Fiona raised her hand again, but this time he grabbed her wrist before she completed the swing. "Perfect," she whispered. "He needs to think we're breaking up."

This was her big plan? It would have been easier to just punch the bouncer and knock him out.

Fiona jerked her arm away and gave her hair an indignant toss as she crossed her arms over her chest and turned her back to Angel. "Just sneak in when his back is turned," she whispered over her shoulder.

Pressing her shoulders back and her chest out, Fiona sauntered toward the bouncer. Angel couldn't hear what they were saying but whatever it was, the bouncer was definitely paying attention. She grabbed the man's tie and pulled him toward her, turning him until his back was to the door.

"I'll be damned," Angel whispered. Staying to the side and watching out for anyone who might be following them, he headed toward the door. He was almost through, and he realized there was no way the bouncer was going to miss him. No way.

The man started to turn and then Fiona, her hand still wrapped in the man's tie, pulled him close and kissed him.

Angel froze in his tracks. The bouncer was a dead man. He'd rip his lips off.

Then Fiona waved at him, motioning him through the door. He caught her gaze. Her eyes were open and despite the kiss, she looked frantic as hell.

He'd hurt the bouncer later.

Angel stepped into the entry and slipped into a dark corner, wishing he could cut the blasting music.

Seconds later, Fiona entered. She waved at the doorman, blew him a kiss and kept walking. Angel fell into step behind her. He leaned in. "Have fun?"

"A big friggin' joy." She wiped her mouth. "But our little friend won't get in."

"What do you mean?"

"I pointed him out to Miguel, the bouncer. I told him that he was my cousin who wanted to take me home and that if he took care of it, I'd make sure it was worth his while." The smile on her mouth went all the way to her eyes. "I know there'll be more men after us, but at least this one isn't getting in and that's one less to worry about. It might buy us a little time."

He loved her optimism. They were on the run. People they cared for were dead. And she'd had to kiss a doorman just to get into a club.

And still, she focused on the bright side of the situation.

He envied that.

Taking her hand in his, he kissed the ring he'd given her, then tilted her chin up and kissed her mouth. She wasn't just beautiful. She was smart.

Damned if he didn't love her.

* * *

Angel kissed her. His gaze was hot and there was something in it she couldn't name, but it made her blush with embarrassment and desire. Neither of which was appropriate, considering their circumstances. She buttoned her shirt and unrolled the waist of her skirt until the cloth fell past her knees once again. Angel was once again all business by the time she finished straightening her clothes. "What next?" she asked, her mouth pressed close to his ear.

"Let's walk," he replied.

Taking her hand, he led her into the club. Salsa lessons were already taking place, and the floor was crowded with couples of varying skill levels. The bar was packed. She imagined the place would be a mob scene of wall-to-wall dancers in a few hours. Quickly, Angel pulled her through the mob and toward the back of the floor.

"Any idea where we're going?" Fiona shouted over the din of music and people.

"We'll start with the back," Angel said. "Look for a door that might lead to the service corridors."

She nodded and turned her attention to escape. A ray of bright light caught her attention, and she saw one of the waiters coming through an open doorway with a tray of glasses. "Over there," Fiona said, pointing toward the opening.

"Let's roll," Angel shouted, quickening his pace.

They skirted the edge of the dance floor, hurrying past a couple dressed in red and black going through a series of whirls and dips.

Beyond them, a man standing at the edge of the floor caught Fiona's attention. He was dressed appropriately, but there was something about the way he looked at them that gave her a chill.

Another member of RADEC? she wondered. Perhaps one of Montoya's men?

Or was she being paranoid?

He smiled at her. It wasn't friendly. *Predatory* was a more accurate description. She'd known the rebels would find them again but a part of her had hoped that her ruse would buy them a few minutes.

"Get in," Angel said.

They were at the employee door. He opened it, and she ducked into it to find a hallway on the other side. The door slammed shut behind them, leaving the hallway in as close to silence as they were likely to get.

"Find something to block the door," Angel ordered. "Something we can run through the handle. A broom. Pipe. Something." Fiona ran down the hall, reading doors. *Conserje.*

Janitor.

Perfect. She opened it, grabbed an industrial-size broom and ran back to Angel.

"Great." Angel jammed it through the handle, angling it to make the door almost impossible to open from the other side.

As if on cue, someone pushed the door. It jammed. There was swearing. Shouting. More pulling on the door. Fiona's mouth went dry.

"Run," Angel said.

She took his hand and they ran down the hallway. A few turns and the hallway dead-ended at a T junction.

"Which way?" Her heart pounded in her ears. The hallway ahead of them stretched a city block with doors on the left that led to restaurants and stores. The doors on the right, she assumed, led to the back of the building.

Neither option sounded safe.

"This way," Angel said, pulling her to the left. Behind them, someone shouted. Whoever was after them must have broken through their makeshift determent.

Angel increased his pace, and Fiona raced to keep up. Ahead

of them, a door on the left opened and a man in white pants, a chef's jacket and hat stepped into the hallway with a garbage bag in his hand.

"Hold it!" Angel shouted.

Surprised, the man held the door as she and Angel hurried in and found themselves in a restaurant kitchen. Dodging waiters and chefs, they hurried into the dining area. Set up to accommodate families with children, it was decorated in garish primary colors and was anything but upscale.

"This'll do," Angel said.

"Do what?" Fiona asked. She pressed her hand to her chest, sure her heart was about to burst.

"Over there," he said, guiding her to a bank of private party rooms.

"Perdón." A waitress stopped them and Fiona held her breath. Was she one of them? Would she say something and blow their cover? *"¿Cómo puedo ayudarle?"*

She wanted to know if she could help them.

Fiona waited for Angel to repond, wondering how he planned to get out of this one.

"La fiesta de cumpleaños de los sobrinos," Angel said, telling her he was looking for his nephew's party.

Fiona tried to slow her breathing and prayed there was a kid with a birthday party in the building. If not, they'd have to leave.

The waitress smiled. *"¿La familia de Gomez o de Valdez?"*

"Valdez," Angel said, smiling and looking more charming than Fiona thought was possible.

"Allá," the waitress said, pointing toward a room on the end.

"Gracias," they both said and headed toward the room.

"Unless you know these people," Fiona whispered. "I can't imagine they'll let us stay."

"I know," Angel agreed, his face drawn with concern. "Just start cleaning the room. Pick up plates. Ask if anyone needs anything. Go slow. We want our tails to get through here and back onto the street. Then we'll head out the back."

"Damned if you aren't the sly one," Fiona said.

"Is that a good thing?" Angel asked.

"It works for me," Fiona said.

They slipped into the room where the birthday party was in full swing with kids running amuck, music blaring and the adults chatting to each other.

Fiona's stomach fell as she realized what they'd done. "If they find us here, we're going to have a huge problem," she said. "I don't like the thought of putting these people, these children, in danger."

Angel frowned. "No choice now. We're here and we can't leave without drawing attention to ourselves." He broke away, mouthing the word *work*.

Fiona skirted the other side of the room. A few heads turned and cast them curious glances until they began to pick up dishes. Dividing her attention between busing tables and listening for their pursuers, in less than a minute she heard voices on the other side of the wall asking if two people had run through the restaurant and then outside.

No. No one, was the answer.

Fiona breathed a sigh of relief and looked to Angel. He nodded and mouthed the words *thirty seconds*.

She ticked off seconds in her head. In thirty, with an armful of dishes, she followed Angel back onto the main floor.

Diners. Waitresses. Waiters.

But no members of RADEC or Montoya's officers caught her eye.

They hurried back to the kitchen, and Fiona reminded herself to act as if she belonged. Forcing herself to remain calm, she set her dishes on the counter next to Angel's then headed to the back door.

She couldn't get out fast enough, and she followed Angel out the door, into the hallway that ran the length of the warehouse and then outside.

The air was cool and she breathed a sigh of relief.

Then the sudden, painful press of cold metal against her head caught her attention. *"Buena tardes, Señorita Macmillan,"* a smug, unfamiliar voice said.

Someone shoved her to the ground. She rolled over just in time to see Angel disarm her assailant with one hand while he punched him in the throat with the other.

The man dropped to his knees next to her, gasping for air.

Angel held out his hand to Fiona. She hesitated, trying to process what had happened.

"Let's go," Angel said. She let him help her to her feet. He wasn't even breathing heavy.

She glanced at the man on the floor. Though she'd never seen such a wound before, she was sure Angel had crushed his windpipe and the man was going to die. From the panic in his eyes, he knew it, as well.

"Don't look," Angel said, trying to shield her eyes.

But she'd seen enough. She shuddered, hearing the man choke and gag as they left.

It was too much. Too fast. She rubbed her eyes with the heels of her palms. "I'm tired of death," she said. "Good men. Bad men. It doesn't matter. I'm just tired."

"He should never have tried to hurt you. He knew the consequences."

A hitch in his voice made her glance up and, for a fleeting moment, she saw regret in his eyes. He'd said he didn't feel guilt, and maybe that was true, but he felt something. She was sure of that.

They reached the dock at midnight and Angel groaned in relief. He was beaten. Tired. And he really wanted his bed.

"Which one is she?" Fiona asked, squinting into the dark.

"There," Angel said. "The Hunter with the red hull."

She squinted harder. "As if I can tell what's red in this light," she muttered.

A dinghy was tied to the dock and Angel quickly unhitched it. "You'll be on her soon enough," he said.

"Isn't someone going to get peeved we're taking their transportation?" Fiona asked as she stepped into the four-man craft.

"We'll have it back by morning," Angel said. The last thing he needed to do was draw attention to himself and Fiona by stealing a boat.

Slowly, he rowed the fifty feet to the *Last Ditch Effort*. It had been over six months since he'd been on her, but he paid the marina to keep the hull clean, check her fluid levels and, if weather rolled in, to make sure she didn't break her moorings.

"How did you manage to keep her a secret?" Fiona asked as they skimmed across the surface of the placid water.

"She's one boat in fifty out here," Angel said. "And there's no reason for anyone to wonder if I have a boat. I'm a mercenary, not a sailor, and until I met you I wasn't exactly a hunted man."

"Oh," Fiona said.

Angel didn't miss the hint of pain in the single word, and mentally slapped himself for being a verbal klutz. He stopped rowing. "I didn't mean it like that."

She hesitated and reached over and squeezed his hand. "It's okay."

And it was okay. He heard that in her voice, as well, and appreciated it, but he needed her to understand how important she was to him. "It's true that when we met, I wasn't a hunted man," he explained. "I was a drunk."

"No," she countered. "You were grieving."

"I was a drunk," he insisted. "With no signs of stopping, and then you came to me for help. In reality, you're the one who saved me." Her hand was still on his, and he brought her knuckles to his lips and kissed them. "Thank you."

"You're welcome," Fiona whispered, her voice tight.

Angel kissed her knuckles again then let go of her hand and picked the oars back up. "So, does that explain why no one knows about my boat?"

"It does," Fiona said, wiping her eyes with the back of her hand.

They reached the *Last Ditch Effort* and Angel tied off the small craft and climbed onboard.

Cautiously, Fiona climbed the ladder then paused at the top. "Permission to come aboard, sir?"

"Permission granted," Angel said.

She stepped onto the deck, wrapped her arms around his waist and rested her head against his chest. "It's over, isn't it?" she asked. "We're safe now, aren't we?"

"We are," Angel said, and an almost tangible weight lifted from his shoulders.

Standing on her toes, she kissed him. "Thank you," she whispered, her mouth against his.

They were home.

"You're welcome," Angel replied, all sense of fatigue disappearing. He'd rest when he was dead.

Turning the combination lock, he opened the hatch and led Fiona downstairs. He sniffed the air. Fresh, with a hint of vanilla. He made a mental note to slip the marina people a few extra dollars.

Rooting in the dark, he found the flashlight he always kept on the ledge just above the table.

Finding it, he flicked it on, eager to show Fiona the boat.

"Angel," Fiona said, her voice hushed as if she were in a church. "She's beautiful."

She was. Made from mahogany, her lines were simple but that was their beauty. Polished chrome glinted in the meager light.

All the curtains were a pale yellow and the cushions of the bench seating were covered to match.

"You should see her under full sail," Angel said, pleased.

"I can't wait," Fiona said.

"You'll have to," Angel said.

Fiona turned to him, an eyebrow raised. "Why?"

"Two reasons. We can't get gas until the morning and we'll need it if we hit a lull." Angel pulled her to him. "And because I want to show you the bedroom."

Fiona grinned. "Why, Captain, are you allowed to fraternize with crew?"

Angel nuzzled her neck. She tasted like salt. "Allowed to fraternize? It's encouraged."

Fiona giggled and Angel picked her up. He couldn't wait. Not right now. Carefully, he slipped to the cabin under the foredeck and tossed Fiona onto the V-shaped bed.

She patted the space next to her. Angel took his shirt off and slid next to her, pulling her shirt up and over her head.

"Make love to me," she whispered.

"That's the plan," he said, tickling her bare skin with the tips of his fingers. "And then we'll have sex."

She laughed again and he grinned. It was good to hear that sound. Taking her mouth, he kissed her hard and she matched him. In seconds, they were both naked.

"Hurry up," Fiona said, stretching beneath him.

"Make me," Angel said, flipping her onto her stomach.

"What are you doing?" she asked, her voice muffled against the pillow.

"This," he said, and slowly ran his hands up her legs, rubbing the muscles.

She groaned in response. "Oh, God, that's good."

"It is," he agreed. He wanted to make love to her but first, he wanted to feel her. Every single smooth inch.

The waves rocked them as he massaged her body, enjoying every groan and sigh of pleasure. Taking a moment, he stretched his back.

"Please, don't stop," Fiona said, her voice sleepy.

Greedy girl.

But she was *his* greedy girl. No one else's. Angel ran his hands up her back, hesitating at her shoulders. "I will never stop touching you," he promised.

Fiona turned over. "Love me," she whispered, wrapping her legs around his hips.

Slowly, Angel sank into her heat, and she hissed in pleasure. He loved her. He knew it. Felt it with every fiber of his being. He took her left hand in his and held it up to the light.

"What?" she asked, smiling.

Her hair was spread over the pillow, and the way she looked at him made him want to kiss her forever.

He liked the feeling. He never wanted that to end. "Marry me," he said.

Her eyes widened. "What?"

Angel took a deep breath. "Last time I waited for the right moment, I lost something precious. The right moment is what we make it. And this—" he kissed her mouth "—you—" he kissed her neck "—this is the right moment. You are the right woman. Marry me."

"Are you sure?"

He leaned back, still inside her. "Say yes."

She smiled. "Yes."

Chapter 15

Heavy footsteps trod on the deck above, waking Fiona. She didn't need to feel for Angel to know he wasn't there. The illuminated clock on the wall showed that it was 1:00 a.m. Scooting to the edge of the bunk, she wrapped the sheet around her body and went outside. She inhaled the cool, salty air, and a yummy sound rolled past her lips.

"I hope that's a happy sound and not a hungry sound," Angel said. "Because there is nothing to eat."

Fiona turned toward his voice. He stood at the bow of the boat.

Careful to keep her balance, she scooted around the few items on deck as she walked toward him. "A happy sound," she assured him. "If I spent the rest of my life on this boat I'd die happy."

Angel chuckled. "We'll see if you feel the same after a few weeks at sea."

She laughed and leaned against the rail. "What are you doing?"

"Taking care of a few things so we can leave," Angel explained. "Putting sails on. Setting coordinates in the autopilot. Things like that."

Fiona leaned against the metal railing. "How long before we sail?" she asked, anxious to get out of Colombia.

"First thing in the morning," Angel said, wrapping a length of rope into a neat swatch. "No one will look for us here."

She gazed over the water. Lights from shore shone on the calm marina water. Above them, stars managed to shine despite the light pollution coming from the city. She imagined that when they were on the open water, the night sky would be stunning. "Is there anything I can do to help?"

Hanging the rope on a hook, he walked over and wrapped his arms around her waist. He was warm, and she snuggled against him. "Would it be wrong if I said that standing there and being pretty was enough?"

She squeezed him. "A little," she said with a low laugh. "But since we're engaged, I'll let it go this time."

He unwrapped her arms and kissed her left hand. "I'll get a different ring if you'd like."

Fiona held her hand out. The fact that the ring was originally meant for someone else should bother her.

Somehow, it didn't. "No. I'm good."

"You sure?" Angel asked, not sounding convinced.

She planted a brief kiss on his mouth. "I might have felt slighted a few weeks ago, but if there's one thing I've learned in Colombia, it's what's important. And we both know life is short." She kissed him again. "What matters is that we don't waste it." She cocked her head. "Does the ring bother *you?*"

"No," he said. "It may sound odd, but I think Isabel would approve." He kissed her again. "Why don't you go get some rest? We'll be leaving at sunrise."

"How about you?" She wiggled her eyebrows. "Coming to bed?"

"After I take care of a few more things. Go." He swatted her bottom and she sauntered below the deck. Crawling back into their bunk, she listened to Angel walking above her as the movement of the boat lulled her.

She was almost asleep when the lack of movement grabbed her attention. She sat up and glanced at the clock. It was 2:00 a.m. How much more could there be to prepping a boat? Perhaps it was selfish, but she wanted him next to her. Once again using the sheet as a robe, she went back on deck.

Angel was nowhere in sight.

"What the hell?" She was sure he hadn't fallen overboard. She'd have heard the splash. A rhythmic sound caught her attention. Angel was in the dinghy, twenty feet from the boat, heading to shore. "Angel?" She called his name, and the rowing stopped.

"Go back to bed," he said as the small craft bobbed in the water.

"Where are you going?" she asked.

"Supplies. Gas."

"At two in the morning?"

"Yes."

Did he think she was an idiot? There were no stores open this late. In NYC? Sure. But in Colombia everything except bars closed after sunset.

She ran through their conversation in her head. *Taking care of a few things,* he'd said. He'd been so nonchalant. So casual.

A much better liar than she realized.

Things meant Montoya. She was sure of it.

"Get back here. Now. I lost Tony to *him*," she said, careful to not say Montoya's name in case there was anyone within earshot. With their distance from the other boats and shore it was doubtful, but still she wasn't taking any chances. "I won't lose you. Not now."

"There's a note. Now go back to bed. I'll be back in a few hours," he said and resumed rowing. She called his name again but he didn't stop until he reached the shore.

Fiona trembled with anger and fear. They were engaged. They were supposed to be a team. Abandoning her to go off on a half-baked trip for revenge was not what a good team member did.

And she'd be damned if she'd put up with it. Tucking in the edge of the sheet to keep it in place, she scanned for the note Angel mentioned and found it on the captain's chair, weighted down with a glass paperweight.

Fiona,

I'm sure you're pissed and have figured out where I'm going, but please understand that I'm doing this for us. Even if you release the tape, Montoya will never leave you alone. He will come after everything and everyone you love.

If I don't return by sunrise, I'm not coming back. There is money in the dresser. Don't bother with the sails. There's gas in the tank. Just get out of here.

I love you.

Angel.

He was right about not being safe, but she'd known that. Montoya was both well funded and well connected, and with that combination, he could buy a hit on her life if he wanted.

But that didn't justify Angel running off half-cocked trying to solve their problem without her. Fiona crumpled the note in her fist. She was going to kill him if Montoya didn't. Of course, she had to find the man first.

What would Angel do? She tapped her chin, thinking.

Maybe he'd send a message to Montoya and find a neutral spot, or perhaps he'd go to Montoya, since Xavier had given up the man's location.

There were too many options.

What she needed was someone who knew Angel and Montoya. Xavier. It all came back to the RADEC leader. If he knew

Montoya's location, it meant he kept tabs on the police chief. And if he kept tabs, then he'd know—or one of his men would know—where Angel was.

Damn it, she was going to have to go back and beg for their help. She really was going to kill Angel after she saved him.

Quickly, she searched the ship for a way to shore, but if there was an inflatable raft of any sort, she couldn't find it.

That left swimming. She pushed her hair back, dreading the prospect of a midnight swim in a marina. She wasn't scared of sharks or any such thing, but there could be trash in the water and getting a foot caught in a loose fishing line could be almost as deadly as tangling with an animal.

Plus, the water was stinky with spilled oil, gas and who knew what else.

She grimaced at the thought, but let the sheet fall to the floor and slipped into her panties, bra and sandals.

Taking a garbage bag from a drawer, she wrapped up the rest of her clothes, a gun recovered from Angel's sock drawer and some of the money Angel had left her.

She picked up the tape of Maria's death. She hated to use it as a bargaining chip, but losing Angel was worse. She kissed the tape and stuck it in the plastic bag. "I'll get you back," she promised. "But first, I get Angel."

"¡Llevame al bar de Rubíes, rápido!" Fiona said, seating herself in the back of the cab.

The cabbie sniffed the air then grimaced. *"Cincuenta pesos."*

Fifty pesos? It was a little steep, but she couldn't blame him. She'd crawled ashore less than ten minutes ago, sputtering and shivering. The water had been colder than she'd thought and trash had floated about like so much flotsam.

Her hair was slimy, and she smelled. She held out the money. *"Gracias."*

He took the bills then gunned the engine.

Settling in the seat, Fiona fought the urge to tug at her wet undergarments and tried to relax. By the time the cabbie pulled to the front of the bar, she was shaking from the heart-pounding ride.

She watched the cab pull away from the curb and the pounding in her chest increased. Slowly, she walked to the front of Rubíes. She could hear voices inside. Low music.

Xavier and his men were still there. It was what she wanted, she reminded herself, but still her heart raced. She put a hand on the door. "For Angel," she said, and pushed it open.

The door swung shut behind her and all talking stopped. Xavier stood up from where he sat at one of the back tables, looking both confused and shocked. "Ms. Macmillan?"

Fiona walked to him and held out the tape. "I need to talk to you."

Wordless, he took the tape then nodded toward the pantry door—the same door the men had come from earlier. Praying she hadn't overestimated her worth, Fiona walked ahead of Xavier and his men.

The room was bigger than she'd assumed, with a side area that had a small table and a few chairs. She took the one closest to the wall and set her gun on the table.

Xavier took the opposite chair, with two men standing behind him and off to each side. His dark eyes curious, he set the tape on the table between them. "First, give me one good reason that I should not put a bullet in your pretty head."

Fiona took a deep breath, calming herself. "Because I'm innocent, and you might be a rebel but I don't think you're a murderer."

Xavier didn't blink but neither did he raise his weapon. Fiona relaxed a notch, relieved she'd read him right.

"What about the tape?" He picked it back up.

"I want you to watch it."

"You said watching it might destroy it."

"It might," she said, hoping she appeared as cool as her captor. "I'll take that chance if you will."

Xavier handed the tape to one of his men. "Get a camera."

Fiona almost sighed with relief. "So, you'll help me?"

"Perhaps, but first we will watch. You will walk out of here alive as long as the tape shows your innocence." Xavier leaned forward, staring at her with black eyes as cold as the water she'd just swum through. "Talk to me while we wait. Tell me, what is it that you want from me?"

Fiona refused to back down. Not until Xavier did what she needed. "Angel has gone to kill Montoya, and I need to find him."

"And this means something to me?" Xavier asked.

"It does. I think you know where Montoya is. If Angel finds Montoya, he will kill him—"

"Good."

"But frankly, I don't think that's good enough," Fiona pressed, letting passion be her persuader.

"Elaborate," Xavier said, his voice surprised.

"Dead is dead. We both know that. There is no justice in death. There is no shame. There is only a political official who will be made a martyr. That helps neither your cause nor mine."

"And what is your cause?" Xavier asked, seeming more interested than he had a few moments ago.

"Angel is my cause. I don't want my fiancé killed trying to protect me."

"Fiancé?"

Fiona held up her hand. "It's official now. He asked. I said yes. Now, you can either help me or not. But I am asking you to please put the good of the cause before your desire for revenge."

"How about the tape? If what you say is true, that Montoya killed Maria, why give it to me?"

Fiona took another breath, hating what she had to do but loving Angel more. "You can keep it—"

Xavier laughed. "That was not up for debate."

"—but if you do, you are a shortsighted fool who doesn't deserve to lead a pack of dogs, much less a group of men."

Xavier stopped laughing. *"¿Perdon?"*

Fiona thought he might jump over the table to smack her, but she couldn't stop if she wanted to. "If you want to win this battle with Montoya and the government, then you will need the support of the world. What better way to win this fight than by giving your story to a reporter who is willing and eager to present your case in a positive light? A reporter who can show the world that Montoya is a monster."

Leaning forward, she took Xavier's hand in hers. "Think of it. Your people will be heroes and the president will have to acknowledge your case. As for Montoya, his career will be over. He will live the rest of his life in shame."

Xavier pulled his hand from hers and crossed his arms over his chest. "I will consider it."

It was a start. "And Angel?"

Xavier rose. "You are right. We have been tracking Montoya. So far, your fiancé has remained out of sight, but if he shows up, we will see him."

Fiona rose. "Then what are we waiting for?"

The man came back in and handed Xavier a camera like the one Tony had used the day of his death. "This," Xavier said, turning it on and watching the small screen.

Fiona held her breath and prayed the tape remained intact.

For a moment, nothing happened. Then light flickered across Xavier's features. She breathed a sigh of relief. She had tried to sound cavalier when handing over the video but deep inside, the thought of losing the footage, after all she and Angel had sacrificed to keep it safe, made her ill.

But not ill enough to keep her from helping Angel. No amount of fame was worth his life.

"Thank God," she murmured then stared, mesmerized by the sound of her last conversation with Tony. There was the gunshot. The one that killed Maria.

Xavier flinched but didn't turn away.

Tony's shout. Another gunshot. Her plea to Tony not to die.

Then nothing. Silence. Again. Just like before. Tears slid down Fiona's cheeks, and she wiped them away with the back of her hands. She hated crying, and crying in front of a stranger even more so.

"It seems you tell the truth about Maria," Xavier said, turning off the recorder.

"Was there ever any doubt?" Fiona sniffed, hating him for putting her through this and wasting time they didn't have.

Once again, Xavier turned pink, but Fiona suspected it was something close to shame. He took her hand in his, helping her to her feet. "Come. Let's go find your fiancé and see if we can keep him from doing something stupid."

Wearing a coat that smelled like beer, month-old sweat and cigarettes, Angel lay sprawled on the sidewalk two houses down from Montoya's local headquarters. Next to him was another drunk and across the street stood a prostitute who, he guessed, had been hooking for about fifty years.

After leaving Fiona, he'd sent the police chief a message by way of a street child, telling Montoya to meet him at a nearby parking lot. There, Angel would give him the tape for Montoya's assurance that he'd leave Fiona alone.

There would be no meeting, though. The moment Montoya stepped outside, Angel was going to put a bullet in his head.

The drunk next to him made a retching sound and Angel tried not to cringe. God, he hated stakeouts. He prayed that Montoya would emerge soon. He'd thought about hitting him from a rooftop, but without a good rifle he didn't want to take the chance on missing the kill shot by using a handgun at a distance.

So playing the drunk was the next best option. And it had the plus side of making this job personal, something that sniping from a roof lacked.

A car pulled up and two men emerged. Angel tensed. Locals or Montoya's men? One walked over and kicked him in the ribs. *"Levántese. Salga de aquí."*

Angel grunted but didn't move. There was no way in hell he was leaving. The man laughed then kicked the other drunk, getting the same lack of reaction Angel had offered.

His partner told him to hurry and the men went inside.

Bastards. Angel tugged his ratty cap over his ears. They'd be lucky if he didn't take them out, as well. He counted the number of times a shadow passed in front of the window of Montoya's house and after thirty minutes, he wondered if he'd overplayed his hand. Where the hell was Montoya? Was he going to hide there all night? The meeting he'd requested was to take place soon.

Another car drove up, parking in front of the building. This one was black. Shiny. A Continental. It had to be Montoya's.

He hoped so. It was late and he wanted to get back to Fiona.

Angel smiled at the thought. Damned if love didn't make him impatient. He took a long, slow, silent breath, reminding himself that when this was over, when Fiona was safe, he'd have all the time he wanted. Time enough for love. For a family.

To find a new line of work.

He looked forward to a new career almost as much as he was looking forward to spending a lifetime with Fiona.

The driver of the Continental emerged and left the car running. Angel stood, adrenaline pumping so fast he shook. Slouched to disguise his height, he staggered down the street. Come on, you bastard. Come out.

Keeping his voice low and gravelly, Angel broke into a slurred

Spanish love song, put his hand in his front jacket pocket and cocked his weapon.

The door opened. Angel held his breath as Montoya emerged with two men in front of him and two behind.

Angel staggered closer, calling attention to himself. *"¡Señor!"* he called. *"Dame un poco de dinero, para que pueda comprar cerveza."*

It was a common question from a drunk: give me money.

Obviously irritated, Montoya turned to him, *"Salga,"* he said, shoving Angel aside as he headed toward the car.

Out of the corner of his eye, he saw one of the men pull his gun. Dammit. He'd hoped that at least two of the guards would get in the car and be out of the way before he had to draw his weapon.

No such luck. Angel pulled his weapon and shot the guard in an area that would incapacitate but not kill. The sound echoed down the empty street, and the man hit the pavement, groaning.

There was a spilt second of collective shock. In that instant, Angel grabbed Montoya, wrapped one arm around the police chief's neck and spun him close while pressing the barrel of his gun to Montoya's head. For a heartbeat, there was nothing but stunned silence, and then clicking sounds as multiple weapons were raised against him.

"¡Alto!" Angel said. *"Tiren sus armas o le disparo."*

The men stopped but didn't drop their guns. "Tell them to drop their weapons," Angel said in Montoya's ear, using him as a shield and waiting to see if any more men would emerge from the building. It remained well lit but silent.

One bit of luck, Angel thought. About time.

"Why?" Montoya answered, not even struggling. "You will kill me if they do that, will you not, *Angel?*"

He had a point.

"I take it the disguise isn't that good," Angel commented, assessing the skill level of the three men. The bigger one was a pro, he was sure of that. The other two looked like kids, barely out of school. He might make it back to the boat alive. Might.

Dammit, he really wanted that life with Fiona.

If he'd had time, he would have planned better. But this was his best chance to make her safe.

Montoya sniffed and made a face. "Your disguise is quite authentic. Nothing I would have done."

Angel knew that was why it had worked. People assumed others would do as they would do. Montoya would never put on such distasteful clothing to kill someone and so assumed that neither would anyone else. "Thanks for saying I'm nothing like you," Angel replied.

"Yes. I am not a coward," Montoya spat. "When I take a life, I look the person in the face. I do not sneak up on them."

Angel rolled his eyes.

But Montoya continued. "I will be a martyr in death. An icon of honor and courage that cannot be ignored." He held his head high, and Angel detected something surprising. *Pride.*

Montoya wasn't lying, Angel realized. He wasn't scared to die, and in fact, welcomed it.

He also wasn't lying about being a martyr. A wave of disappointment washed over Angel as he realized that he couldn't kill the bastard. If he did, he'd be giving Montoya everything he wanted and screwing over RADEC at the same time.

As much as he hated the thought, he'd have to let Montoya live. Still, he could hurt him in the best way possible—let Fiona do her job and bring him to his metaphorical knees in front of the world he was so eager to impress.

He gripped Montoya. Of course, it would have been better to figure that out prior to putting himself in this situation. Angel eyed the still-running car.

"Need a hand?" a feminine voice asked, stepping from the shadows.

Fiona?

The three men turned as she approached but none moved. Behind her was a party of ten RADEC rebels.

Damned if she hadn't brought the cavalry.

"You are going to make a great wife," he said as Fiona's contingent of men disarmed Montoya's group and Xavier put his gun on Montoya, giving Angel the chance to step back.

"Thanks. I thought you might be in a bit of a jam."

Angel shrugged. "I was fine."

"Liar," Fiona countered.

Angel rolled his eyes, and she gave a nod in Montoya's direction. "We need to talk about this."

"About Montoya?" Angel eyed the police chief. "I have some thoughts—"

"Me first," Fiona said, cutting him off. "I know he's a monster and doesn't deserve to breathe, but you can't kill him."

Angel opened his mouth to tell her that he'd come to the same conclusion, but she seemed so passionate, he let her speak instead. "I'll tell you what I told Xavier. Dead is dead. If we let him live, he'll live in shame and probably in jail. That's much worse than death."

Angel grinned. This was her moment and there was no way he was taking it away from her. "You're right."

She took a step back. "Really? You agree?"

He shrugged. "You make a compelling case, but I do have one thing I want to say." He turned back to Montoya. "You don't think about Fiona. You don't breathe her name to anyone. If anything happens to her, *anything,* I will kill you. It won't be fast, and by the time I am finished with you, you will beg for death. Any death."

"Scum," Montoya said, his mouth curled in a sneer. "No one will believe you. No one. And when you are discredited as the liars you are, I will be the winner."

"Idiot," Angel sighed.

"I am a great man and I live for—"

"Xavier, will you please shut him up," Angel said, interrupting.

Grinning, Xavier thumped Montoya on the head with the butt of his gun. Montoya wavered on his feet and Xavier hit him again. Montoya dropped to the sidewalk in a heap.

"You sure you want him to live?" Xavier asked, nudging the unconscious man with his foot.

"The lady calls the shots, Xavier," Angel said. "And if she can convince you to do what she wants, I'm sure she can hold Montoya up to the world and make them see what he truly is."

"About that," Xavier stepped over Montoya. "In the matter of the tape, we want to give it back."

"You have it?" Angel asked, surprised. "When the hell did that happen?"

"She traded it for our help saving you." He fished the cassette from his pocket and handed it to Fiona. "We trust you to do as you promised."

Fiona put the tape in her pocket. "I won't let you down."

Angel watched the transaction, shaken to his soul. He knew she was capable of sacrifice, but the tape was more than he'd have expected of anyone—especially a talented, driven reporter. "What the hell did I ever do to deserve you?" he asked, pulling Fiona close.

She wrinkled her nose and turned her head. "Honey, you smell."

Angel chuckled and took off the hat and coat.

She sniffed and raised a brow. "Better."

"Liar," he said, kissing her mouth.

"I prefer to think of it as diplomatic," she said with a smile.

Damn, he loved her. Tilting her head up, he placed a quick kiss on his mouth. She tasted like life. Like the future.

Their future.

Chapter 16

Fiona raked a hand through her short blond hair. The cut was cute in an athletic way, but not her, she thought with a sigh.

"Your hair is perfect, Mrs. Castillo," a familiar voice said.

Fiona jumped, turning in her chair. "You're not supposed to be here. This is the green room. Are you trying to get me in trouble?"

"You worry too much." Angel smiled and walked into the room, shutting the door behind him.

Fiona turned back to the mirror, watching him as he came toward her. Coming up behind her, he kissed the side of her neck. "And for the record, I like your hair no matter what the length."

"But you prefer it long," Fiona said.

He kissed the opposite side of her neck. It was six months since they'd left Colombia and three months since their wedding aboard the *Last Ditch Effort,* and his kisses still made her shiver. "I'm a guy. I will always prefer long hair," he said. "You could have short hair. Long hair. Gray hair. *Black* hair. And I'd love you the same."

She turned in his arms. "Black hair? Do you feel the urge to dye something?"

He kissed her forehead. "I do miss those Groucho Marx eyebrows."

"Say that again and I might just go back to them," Fiona said in mock anger.

Angel laughed and kissed her again, making her toes curl. "How did I get so lucky," she murmured against his mouth.

"No idea," he replied. "Right place. Right time."

"Meeting you was the only right thing about Colombia." She rested her head against his chest.

"Nervous?" Angel asked.

"A little," she admitted. She'd already won an Emmy Award for her story, and while it was an honor to receive the award, she couldn't look at it without thinking of Tony and Maria and all who'd died.

Angel pulled up a chair and sat next to her. "I have something that might make you a little less nervous."

"If it involves getting me naked, I'm not sure we have time for that," Fiona joked. Though she had to admit that making love with Angel always managed to calm her.

Angel rolled his eyes. "And they say men have only one thing on their minds." He pulled a letter from his pocket and opened it. "It's from Xavier."

"How's he doing?"

"Better," said Angel

Fiona frowned. Since Montoya's conviction and subsequent disappearance, the Colombian government was just beginning to broach changes. She had hoped her film of Maria's and Tony's death would give the wheels of political change a bit more grease, but she soon found out that change took more than one tape.

Still, changes were occurring, and the leaders of RADEC were in negotiation with the Colombian president. That was something.

"What does he say?" Fiona asked. "Are the negotiations going well?"

"He says they are but he isn't part of them."

Fiona straightened. "What? Why not?"

Angel shrugged and handed her the letter. "He says he's a fighter. Not a politician."

Fiona took the letter and scanned it. It elaborated on Angel's explanation. Xavier saw the ongoing problems in Colombia and was now working to help recover kidnap victims.

He also wanted to know if she would mention the cause and the need for help in one of her broadcasts or in an article. She folded the paper and slid it into her purse.

"Well?" Angel asked.

She smiled. "Of course, I'll say something. I'm as frustrated as he is, as we all are, with the lack of progress."

Angel took her hands in his. "You did good, Fiona. Change may not be happening as fast as you want, but it is happening."

Someone knocked on her door and a voice called out, "Three minutes, Ms. Castillo."

Fiona sat up and took a deep breath. "How do I look?"

"Amazing," Angel said. "But you always do."

"Thanks," she said, swallowing to force the butterflies into submission. "Jeez, I'm going to talk to Larry King," she said. "He's an icon, for pity's sake."

Angel kissed the top of her head. "We can always skip it. Go to dinner instead."

"I'm not that nervous," she insisted then cast him a sideways glance. "You know, he might have a few questions for you about what happened and how it plays into the new movie."

Angel shrugged. "I doubt it. It's not a big deal."

"It is to me," she said. Using his experience in Colombia and as a mercenary, Angel had parlayed himself a consultant position on a new action movie. It was his first gig using his skill set for something other than mercenary work, and the studio liked him so much that she was sure it wouldn't be his last.

"I know," he replied. "But this is about you and what happened. Let's keep it simple."

"I suppose. Still, he might be curious." She tugged at his shirt. "You might want to consider changing into a button-down. I know you have a black one," she teased. His penchant for black had turned into a running joke since they'd returned to the States. It didn't help that his consultant job only reinforced the "tough guy who only wears black" persona.

"One? I have four," Angel said, helping her from the chair. "Come on. I'll walk you."

Slipping her shoes on, Fiona took one last look at her outfit. Perfect skirt. Perfect shirt. Perfect hair.

But the face, she decided, was different. Older. Wiser.

And happier.

Angel offered her his arm. She slipped hers through it then leaned up to kiss him on the cheek. "My hero."

* * * * *

Turn the page for a sneak preview of
AFTERSHOCK, *a new anthology*
featuring New York Times *bestselling author*
Sharon Sala.

Available October 2008.

n o c t u r n e ™

Dramatic and sensual tales of paranormal romance.

Chapter 1

October
New York City

Nicole Masters was sitting cross-legged on her sofa while a cold autumn rain peppered the windows of her fourth-floor apartment. She was poking at the ice cream in her bowl and trying not to be in a mood.

Six weeks ago, a simple trip to her neighborhood pharmacy had turned into a nightmare. She'd walked into the middle of a robbery. She never even saw the man who shot her in the head and left her for dead. She'd survived, but some of her senses had not. She was dealing with short-term memory loss and a tendency to stagger. Even though she'd been told the problems were most likely temporary, she waged a daily battle with depression.

Her parents had been killed in a car wreck when she was twenty-one. And except for a few friends—and most recently her boyfriend, Dominic Tucci, who lived in the apartment right above hers, she was alone. Her doctor kept reminding her that she should be grateful to be alive, and on one level she knew he was right. But he wasn't living in her shoes.

If she'd been anywhere else but at that pharmacy when the robbery happened, she wouldn't have died twice on the way to the hospital. Instead of being grateful that she'd survived, she couldn't stop thinking of what she'd lost.

But that wasn't the end of her troubles. On top of everything else, something strange was happening inside her head. She'd begun to hear odd things: sounds, not voices—at least, she didn't think it was voices. It was more like the distant noise of rapids—a rush of wind and water inside her head that, when it came, blocked out everything around her. It didn't happen often, but when it did, it was frightening, and it was driving her crazy.

The blank moments, which is what she called them, even had a rhythm. First there came that sound, then a cold sweat, then panic with no reason. Part of her feared it was the beginning of an emotional breakdown. And part of her feared it wasn't—that it was going to turn out to be a permanent souvenir of her resurrection.

Frustrated with herself and the situation as it stood, she upped the sound on the TV remote. But instead of *Wheel of Fortune,* an announcer broke in with a special bulletin.

"This just in. Police are on the scene of a kidnapping that occurred only hours ago at The Dakota. Molly Dane, the six-year-old daughter of one of Hollywood's blockbuster stars, Lyla Dane, was taken by force from the family apartment. At this time they have yet to receive a ransom demand. The housekeeper was seriously injured during the abduction, and is, at the present time, in surgery. Police are hoping to be able to talk to her once she regains consciousness. In the meantime, we are going now to a press conference with Lyla Dane."

Horrified, Nicole stilled as the cameras went live to where the actress was speaking before a bank of microphones. The shock and terror in Lyla Dane's voice were physically painful to watch. But even though Nicole kept upping the volume, the sound continued to fade.

Just when she was beginning to think something was wrong with her set, the broadcast suddenly switched from the Dane press conference to what appeared to be footage of the kidnapping, beginning with footage from inside the apartment.

When the front door suddenly flew back against the wall and four men rushed in, Nicole gasped. Horrified, she quickly realized that this must have been caught on a security camera inside the Dane apartment.

As Nicole continued to watch, a small Asian woman, who she guessed was the maid, rushed forward in an effort to keep them out. When one of the men hit her in the face with his gun, Nicole moaned. The violence was too reminiscent of what she'd lived through. Sick to her stomach, she fisted her hands against her belly, wishing it was over, but unable to tear her gaze away.

When the maid dropped to the carpet, the same man followed with a vicious kick to the little woman's midsection that lifted her off the floor.

"Oh, my God," Nicole said. When blood began to pool beneath the maid's head, she started to cry.

As the tape played on, the four men split up in different directions. The camera caught one running down a long marble hallway, then disappearing into a room. Moments later he reappeared, carrying a little girl, who Nicole assumed was Molly Dane. The child was wearing a pair of red pants and a white turtleneck sweater, and her hair was partially blocking her abductor's face as he carried her down the hall. She was kicking and screaming in his arms, and when he slapped her, it elicited an agonized scream that brought the other three running. Nicole watched in horror as one of them ran up and put his hand over Molly's face. Seconds later, she went limp.

One moment they were in the foyer, then they were gone.

Nicole jumped to her feet, then staggered drunkenly. The bowl of ice cream she'd absentmindedly placed in her lap shattered at her feet, splattering glass and melting ice cream everywhere.

The picture on the screen abruptly switched from the kidnapping to what Nicole assumed was a rerun of Lyla Dane's plea for her daughter's safe return, but she was numb.

Before she could think what to do next, the doorbell rang. Startled by the unexpected sound, she shakily swiped at the tears and took a step forward. She didn't feel the glass shards piercing her feet until she took the second step. At that point, sharp pains shot through her foot. She gasped, then looked down in confusion. Her legs looked as if she'd been running through mud, and she was standing in broken glass and ice cream, while a thin ribbon of blood seeped out from beneath her toes.

"Oh, no," Nicole mumbled, then stifled a second moan of pain.

The doorbell rang again. She shivered, then clutched her head in confusion.

"Just a minute!" she yelled, then tried to sidestep the rest of the debris as she hobbled to the door.

When she looked through the peephole in the door, she didn't know whether to be relieved or regretful.

It was Dominic, and as usual, she was a mess.

Nicole smiled a little self-consciously as she opened the door to let him in. "I just don't know what's happening to me. I think I'm losing my mind."

"Hey, don't talk about my woman like that."

   Nicole rode the surge of delight his words brought. "So I'm still your woman?"
   Dominic lowered his head.
   Their lips met.
   The kiss proceeded.
   Slowly.
   Thoroughly.

* * * * *

Be sure to look for the
AFFTERSHOCK *anthology next month,*
as well as other exciting paranormal stories
from Silhouette Nocturne.
Available in October wherever books are sold.

Silhouette®

nocturne™

NEW YORK TIMES BESTSELLING AUTHOR

SHARON SALA

JANIS REAMES HUDSON
DEBRA COWAN

———

AFTERSHOCK

Three women are brought to the brink of death...
only to discover the aftershock of their trauma has
left them with unexpected and unwelcome gifts of
paranormal powers. Now each woman must learn to
accept her newfound abilities while fighting for life,
love and second chances....

Available October wherever books are sold.

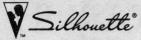

Romantic
SUSPENSE

**Sparked by Danger,
Fueled by Passion.**

USA TODAY bestselling author

Merline Lovelace

Undercover Wife

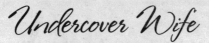

Secret agent Mike Callahan, code name Hawkeye,
objects when he's paired with sophisticated
Gillian Ridgeway on a dangerous spy mission
to Hong Kong. Gillian has secretly been in love
with him for years, but Hawk is an overprotective
man with a wounded past that threatens to
resurface. Now the two must put their lives—
and hearts—at risk for each other.

Available October wherever books are sold.

Silhouette®
Romantic
SUSPENSE

COMING NEXT MONTH

#1531 UNDERCOVER WIFE—Merline Lovelace
Code Name: Danger

Rough around the edges Mike Callahan, code name Hawkeye, objects when he's paired with sophisticated Gillian Ridgeway on a dangerous spy mission to Hong Kong. Hawk is an overprotective man with a wounded past, and Gillian has secretly been in love with him for years. Now the two must put their lives—and hearts—at risk for each other.

#1532 RANCHER'S REDEMPTION—Beth Cornelison
The Coltons: Family First

Rancher Clay Colton discovers a wrecked car and a bag of money on his property, so the local police call in a CSI team—headed by his ex-wife, Tamara. As she investigates, the two are thrown into the path of danger, uncovering secrets about the crime as well as their true feelings for each other.

#1533 TERMS OF SURRENDER—Kylie Brant
Alpha Squad

Targeted by a bank robber bent on revenge, hostage negotiators and former lovers Dace Recker and Jolie Conrad are reunited against their will. The FBI has recruited them to draw out the killer, but their close proximity to each other will draw out wounds from their past. Can they heal their hearts for a second chance at love?

#1534 THE DOCTOR'S MISSION—Lyn Stone
Special Ops

When Dr. Nick Sandro is recruited to help COMPASS agent Cate Olin recover after a head injury, his mission is complicated by the feelings they still harbor for each other. Escaping to Tuscany as a terrorist sends men after Cate, Nick must do all he can to protect her. But they'll have to work together to destroy the final threat.